BEYOND THE GRILL

Tracey Michael

Dedicated to Vin Diesel and Paul Walker. The real love they had for each other as brothers was in every moment they shared on and off the screen. It was truly inspiring.

THE MUSICAL sound of another life terminated pulled Justin from the distraction across the mall, but he kept looking back. They were holding hands, laughing, mooning over each other. It would have been disgusting if it didn't hurt so much. Paul, Jake, Ralph—whatever his name—had never done that with Justin. The most disturbing part of the whole situation was Justin's lack of surprise. He'd known it was nothing more than hooking up, scratching an itch, a way to kill time.

Sighing, he turned his attention back to the game. He glanced at Shane, who gave him a concerned look. Justin shook his head and wrapped his hand around the joystick. "Let's just play."

"This is your last life," Shane said. "I have tokens in my jacket. Help yourself so you don't have to start over."

"Thanks," Justin said, smiling his gratitude. Every time they played, Shane kicked his ass at Street Fighter until Justin ran out of tokens. He stuck his hand in Shane's pocket and pulled out more tokens.

Justin and Shane sometimes hung out at the same arcade, one of a half dozen on the east side of Chicago. Situated inside the mall, this one was by far the nicest. Nine times out of ten, they ended up playing against each other. Once in a while, their group of mutual friends would meet up and go to a movie or out for burgers. Over the last few months, however, the size of the group had dwindled to a lonely few as the others found their other halves. Justin glanced across the food court again. He might not be surprised by the way Randy—that was his name—acted, but he was a little surprised by the sex of his companion. What a wonderful way to start the new year.

One Friday night toward the end of March, Justin's shift was ending at Jerry's Burgers when Shane came for a sandwich.

"Did ya stop to see me?" Justin asked.

"No. I was hungry."

"Uh-huh. Sure." Justin had no clue what made him flirt. For the fun of it, he guessed. And possibly too much caffeine. He gave Shane an exaggerated wink. "I think you want to buy me dinner to make up for making me play against the computer at the arcade."

"What? No one else will share their tokens with you?" Shane tried to look sympathetic, but he wasn't pulling it off. "I've been busy at the garage."

"Work is a rotten excuse for not being there to bail me out." Justin pouted.

"I have to work or I won't have money to buy tokens... or gas... or you dinner."

Was Shane flirting back? No.... He liked girls. Shane

always had girls hanging around him. Besides, even if Shane liked guys, he was way out of Justin's league. The thought made Justin falter, and his smile felt a bit more forced than it had been the moment before. "That is true. I suppose I can forgive you."

"Something wrong?" Shane asked.

"No, just tired. I'm good." Justin smiled.

"Ah, okay." Shane grabbed the bag with his burger inside and turned toward the door. "See you later, Justin."

After Justin clocked out, he walked to his car. The rules stated he had to park across the lot so the customers could be near the door. The problem with working at night meant his car was mostly in the dark. Justin noticed a vehicle next to his, but it didn't freak him out. Other employees parked in that area. But then he saw the dark head above his driver's door. He couldn't see the guy's face, only the hairless scalp.

Who is that, and why are they leaning against my car? He kept moving but more cautiously.

After Justin rounded the back of his car, the man turned toward him, the corner of his mouth lifted in a half smile. Relieved and a little curious, Justin returned his smile. "What are you doing?" Justin asked.

"Waiting for you," Shane smirked.

"Um, I noticed that part. Why are you waiting for me?" It wouldn't be the first time Justin flirted with the wrong man and ended up being taught a lesson.

Shane shrugged. "Because I wanted to. Do you have somewhere you need to be?"

"Not really. I was going to grab something to eat, but it can wait."

"You didn't eat while you were here?" Shane asked.

Shane cocked his head to the side, and Justin's heart did

this funny jumpy thing. "Nah. I'm kinda tired of the food here. I was heading uptown to see whose line was the shortest."

"Denny's is around the corner. I could follow you over there, if you want," Shane offered. "It's getting late, but they're open for the drinking crowd."

"I could go for some eggs...." Justin nodded and then opened the door of his '69 Mustang. It was white and primer gray, and the door creaked when it opened and closed. Justin turned his face away, embarrassed by his ride for the first time. He was working on the car, restoring it bit by bit, but lack of time and money delayed its completion. He only allocated so much of his check to car maintenance.

I bet his door doesn't make noise when it opens.

"I'll meet you over there," Shane said. Justin watched Shane look over his car as he left.

Justin got into his car, and on the first hit of the key, the engine fired brilliantly with a healthy rumble. He had finished the motor; since it wouldn't do him much good to have a nice-looking car if it didn't run, that had been his first priority.

The witching hour was approaching. Traffic was light on the outskirts of town, and luck had him catching both green lights. Justin pulled into the parking spot beside Shane and cut his engine. He checked his hair in the rearview mirror, then prayed he hadn't been seen checking. He climbed out and moved to the back of his car. Shane waited against the bumper of his '69 Dodge Challenger.

"Must be our lucky night," Justin said.

"What makes you say that?" He grinned.

"We made both green lights, and this parking lot is mostly empty. We should be able to get a table fast."

"Ah. Okay. Well, let's get inside and get you fed. I'd hate to see you waste away." Shane laughed.

Justin's hand automatically went to his stomach. It was threatening to rumble, one of the hazards of working fast food and smelling greasy hamburgers all night. He was either starving when he got off work or not interested in food at all. Tonight he was starving.

He followed Shane into Denny's, and the hostess seated them right away. They turned down the coffee she offered and ordered sodas instead.

"Your car sounds tough. Who did the motor?" Shane asked.

"I did. It took me a few weeks to scrape together enough cash, but I wanted top of the line under the hood." Justin was proud of his car, when it wasn't making embarrassing noises in front of good-looking men.

Shane looked impressed. "I can tell. She was purring. How's the outside coming?"

"Uh, well, slow. Making the outside look good takes more time than I've had lately," Justin told him.

"If you ever want some help, give me a yell. I like doing body work," Shane said.

Justin's mind went straight into the gutter. He forced the thought away, though. "Thanks. I'll keep you in mind."

The waitress came over and took their order, then disappeared around the wall dividing the dining room from the kitchen. He watched her go just so he didn't keep staring at Shane. When Justin couldn't see her anymore, he turned his head to find Shane studying him. "What?" Justin asked.

"You surprise me."

"How's that?"

"I never would have taken you for a gearhead." Shane

smiled. "And you just ordered enough food to feed us both. Do you always eat like that?"

Justin felt his cheeks heat, and he shifted in his seat. Dropping his chin, he looked down at his napkin-wrapped silverware on the table. He picked at the corner of his silverware, peeling the layers apart so he wouldn't have to look at Shane. "Depends on the night, I guess."

"Hey. What's wrong?"

"Nothing. Why?" Justin said, head still down.

"Maybe because you're staring at your silverware like it's got a story to tell."

He raised his head and looked at Shane. His cheeks had cooled, and he gave Shane a half smile. "Maybe it did."

Shane's eyes moved over Justin's face for a minute. He apparently decided Justin was cool because he returned the smile. "How long you been slinging burgers around the corner?"

"Since I was sixteen. I'm a shift supervisor now." Justin didn't want to brag, but he'd worked his ass off to move up.

"That's cool."

"Yeah. It pays the bills and then some. I'd like to pick up something else part-time, but I don't have enough free time as it is."

"You could come work for me when you do have time," Shane offered.

"You don't know what I can do and you're offering me a job?" Justin was stunned. *Why would he do that?*

"I've heard what you did with the motor under your hood. A novice couldn't do that. Anything you don't know how to do, I'll teach you."

"I'll think about it. Thanks." A genuine smile curved

Justin's lips this time. "So business at your garage is good, then?"

"Yeah, I'm pretty steady lately. Spring and summer is when I'm usually busiest. People get their vehicles ready for vacations about this time of year."

The waitress brought Justin's food, and he saw what Shane had been teasing him about. He had ordered enough food for both of them. Justin pushed the plate into the middle of the table and nodded toward it. "Dig in. I can't eat all this myself. Well, I probably could, but then I'd have to walk home so I don't lose my girlish figure." Justin winked at him and dug into the fries.

Shane laughed and picked up the ketchup. "You crack me up."

"Why, thank you."

They talked long after the last fry disappeared. Shane told Justin about his family. His mother, who was half-black, had raised him alone after his Hispanic father left them. Shane had been too young to understand at the time. His love for the woman who raised him showed on his face and sounded in his voice while he talked about her. She wouldn't speak ill of the man who'd abandoned them and wouldn't allow Shane to either. It was obvious he'd made peace with the choice his father made a long time ago, since there wasn't any bitterness in his demeanor.

Justin told a very different story of his schoolteacher parents. His father still substituted at the high school since his retirement, while his mother was in her last year of teaching before she retired also.

The clock read the wee hours of the morning by the time they paid and made their way out to the parking lot and their rides. Somehow during the course of the meal, while talking and laughing, he'd gotten Shane's phone number added to his contacts list in his cell.

Justin turned to face him when they reached the back of his car and froze. *What do I do now? Shake his hand, punch his arm, pat his shoulder?* Man, he was no good at this stuff.

He needn't have worried, though, because Shane walked around to the driver's side door and glanced his way. "You mind?"

"No. Go ahead."

Shane opened the door and ducked his head inside. He didn't look around long; there wasn't much to see. "You're getting there, slow but sure."

"Yeah. It'll be great when it's done."

Shane shoved his hand out, and Justin took it. Then Shane pulled him into one of those guy hugs and slapped him on the back. Justin got a nose full of his cologne, and there was instant wood in his jeans. *Ah hell.* He was destined to fuck up another friendship by being attracted to the friend. *Shit.*

2

F ROM INSIDE his car, Shane watched Justin pull out of the parking lot. A smile curved his lips as he shook his head, trying to reconcile the outside of the car with the monster rumble under the hood. Justin had done a stellar job on the motor. Shane couldn't wait to see what the car looked like when he finished it.

He backed from his parking space and drove toward home. His fingers drummed on the steering wheel in time with the music pumping from the speakers, but he couldn't tell anyone what song played. His attention was focused on the man he'd just parted company with. He had no clue where the bug in his ass had come from that made him drive over to wait for Justin to get off work.

Shane had been sitting on the back deck of his house, drinking a soda and staring off into space when the image of Justin with his wild curls floated by his mind's eye. Once he started thinking of Justin, he'd realized he hadn't seen him in a couple of weeks. The last Shane heard, Justin worked at the fast-food joint.

The next thing he knew, he was driving in the direction of the restaurant. Anxiety drove him from his car to go in and order a burger so he could see Justin. After the banter at the counter, Shane hesitated to climb into his car and leave. Instead, he unwrapped his sandwich and leaned against his car door while he ate it. He shifted position, going from leaning against his own car to sitting behind the wheel. After a half-dozen songs played on the radio, Shane got out and walked to stand on the other side of his ride. He leaned against the car parked beside his to think. Justin had never teased him before. It felt like flirting. He'd be happy if that's what it was. Spending time with Justin at the arcade or when they hung out with their friends made it hard to get to know him, but Shane felt some connection, especially tonight. He'd decided on giving him another half hour before walking inside, when Justin had come out. Seeing the uncertainty and curiosity on Justin's face when he realized Shane was waiting for him had done something to Shane's chest. He longed to pull Justin in for a hug to wipe the insecurity away. Suggesting a late sit-down dinner had been a spur of the moment decision. Shane really had no reason to be there, but damned if he would leave without at least a conversation.

It turned out to be a great suggestion. Hours had passed like minutes with them talking and laughing. He was still patting himself on the back as he pulled in front of his house.

After locking his car, Shane walked up the sidewalk and to the front door. Normally the quiet was a welcome change to the noise of working on cars all day. Tonight, though, after spending time with Justin, he wished he at least had a dog to come home to.

Justin had surprised him at every turn. Shane had him

pegged as the shy, geeky type. Who would have guessed a gearhead existed under that fast-food uniform?

Shane pulled out his cell and called the number for the parts store. "Yeah, it's Shane. I need a car stereo, the good one with the CD player and iPod hookup. I need speakers to fit a '69 Mustang too. Oh, and four door bushings for the same car." He hung up after leaving the message.

The uncertainty and insecurities Justin kept inside bothered Shane. He noticed it when they played video games at the arcade. The way Justin kept his head down when strangers stopped by to talk to Shane spoke volumes. But the biggest giveaway was the deflated way Justin sat when Shane teased him. Shane never meant to poke fun in a malicious way, but maybe someone from Justin's past had.

The man was smart, gorgeous, driven, and gorgeous. Did he think that already? Justin shouldn't be insecure about anything. Shane grinned to himself. Justin smelled good too —under the stale-fry-and-greasy-hamburger scent lingered something musky and masculine. The feel of Justin against his body had made Shane's dick twitch.

Shane frowned when he noticed a strange smell. It wasn't an offensive scent, just unusual. He lifted his shirt to his nose and sniffed. Hamburgers. He grinned. Justin. Gripping the back of his T-shirt, he hauled it over his head as he made his way to his bedroom. After dropping the shirt in his hamper, he finished undressing and lay down on the bed. Staring at the ceiling, Shane slid his hand down his smooth chest, down past his ripped abs, and fisted his limp cock. He started pulling until he felt it harden, and stroking from the base to the tip, he closed his eyes. Shane moaned Justin's name, imagining what the man would look like flushed with passion, eyes burning with desire. For him. He pumped harder and faster, then threw his head back against the pillows and growled as his seed coated his hand.

Justin drove home with the memories of the night playing like a movie in his mind. He smiled when he remembered watching Shane laugh. He found himself laughing aloud. The sound startled him in the quiet of the car. Damn, he really needed to get a radio in here.

Witty retorts and more interesting responses came to him as he thought back over their conversation. *Why couldn't I have thought of them sooner?* But he figured he'd held his own pretty well.

When Justin pulled into his driveway, he turned off the car and sat for a minute before getting out and heading to his front door. He unlocked the door, and silence greeted him. Shaking off the loneliness, he closed the door behind him. He clapped his hands together twice, and the lights in the living room came to life. The Clapper, not just for the elderly anymore.

As he made his way through the quiet room, he found the remote for his iPod dock and flipped on something low-key. It was nearly 3:00 a.m., and he was too wound up to sleep at the moment. He sat down on the couch, and five minutes later, he opened his eyes to the sun shining in his face.

Only it hadn't been five minutes. He'd passed out for hours.

Justin used the heel of his hand to rub the sleep from his eyes and stood up. After a quick stop in the bathroom for a piss, he went out to the kitchen to raid the fridge. He didn't look for food; his stomach was still full from the midnight meal. He found a lone bottle of Pepsi on the shelf and unscrewed the lid. He tipped the bottle up while he guzzled, then wandered back to the bathroom for a shower. He'd fallen asleep in his uniform from the night before. He felt gross, and even though he was planning to spend a couple of hours in his garage before he went back to work, he couldn't stand to smell himself. His work clothes needed washing too.

He turned on the hot water and leaned back against the counter. Steam billowed up from the bottom of the tub. Justin watched the cloud spread through the bathroom. He set the half-empty bottle of Pepsi on the counter and started peeling his stained, smelly clothes from his body. Once he was naked, he leaned over, adjusted the water temperature, and pulled the diverter up to start the shower. He stepped in and pulled the curtain closed. The hot water hit his back, and he felt the goosebumps sprout on his skin before he got used to the temperature. Tilting his head back, he let the water soak his short sandy blond curls.

When his hair was squeaky clean, Justin started washing his body. He paid attention to the dips and curves of his lean frame. His sculpted pecs and six-pack abs were sprinkled with light brown hair.

Justin made a point of taking care of his body, exercising and eating right. Well, most of the time. Pepsi and the occasional fast food were his only vices. He didn't smoke and rarely drank. On the occasions he spent time with friends, he allowed himself two drinks. Getting liquored up and making an ass of himself didn't enthuse him in the least. He was perfectly capable of doing that without alcohol.

His shower finished, Justin shut off the water and climbed out. He lifted his hand to the glass of the mirror and wiped a clear spot from the fog. His green eyes stared back at him, vivid in the paleness of his skin. He really needed a vacation on a beach, somewhere he could lay about and put color into his skin. Relaxing with someone special. Yeah, he could get into that in a big way.

Justin wrapped the towel around his waist and opened the bathroom door. His bedroom door stood open across from him. He walked the three steps into the room. The bed was messy and tossed, giving the illusion of someone having a very good time. At least that's what it looked like to him. Wishful thinking at its finest. He was to the point where he'd give his left nut for freaking cuddle time.

He spun on his heel and went back to get his dirty clothes from the bathroom. Wandering down the hall with his arms full, he was grateful for the tidiness his mom had instilled in him. Tripping over crap with his hands full and wearing only a towel would have sucked. With his luck, he'd end up facedown in the hall with his ass in the air.

His phone fell from his pants pocket halfway to the washer. Good thing too or he might have washed it. The little green light at the top blinked at him from the floor.

"I'll be with you in one second," Justin said. He stepped over the phone and continued on to the laundry room.

Probably work. Who called off this time? One of the downsides of hiring teenagers was that a lot of them hadn't learned a work ethic yet.

If I put my clothes in the washer, I can't go in early. He smiled at his own logic.

Justin dumped his uniforms in the washer, started the water, and then dumped in the detergent. After he closed the lid, he went back to pick up his phone. He pushed the button on the side to bring up the screen. He had one missed call. Whoever it was had left a message, though. He debated ignoring the voice mail, but he had his excuse for work, so he might as well listen.

Shane's voice sounded rougher than it had last night. "Good morning. I have something for you if you have time to stop by before work." Justin heard him yawn and then leave his address. "Let me know."

The voice mail lady told him to press one to listen again, two if he wanted to save it, seven to delete. He chose two and closed his phone. Justin was surprised Shane contacted him so soon. His worries over not being interesting enough seemed to be unfounded if Shane was calling him already. He calculated the washer and dryer time to completion and how long he'd have before his shift started. *Plenty of time.*

Justin paced the hallway while he waited for Shane to answer his cell. When Shane's voice came through the speaker, it was clearer than it had been on the voice mail. "Hello."

"Hey. I got your message. Sorry. I was in the shower when you called," Justin responded.

"Oh. Good. I just got up, and you were on my mind." Justin could hear the smile in Shane's voice. He also heard an innuendo, but that could have been his imagination.

"You were on mine when I woke up too." Justin rolled his eyes and shook his head. "Anyway, you said you had something for me?"

"Yeah. Do you have time to stop by before you go to work?"

"I have to wait for my clothes to finish washing and drying. Then I can come."

"I can bring it over, if you want," Shane offered.

"You don't have somebody's ride you need to work on?" Justin asked.

"That's the beauty of working for myself. I can do it when I want. What's your address?"

Justin gave it to him and went to flop down on the couch. "I don't mind stopping on my way to work."

"What's the matter? Your place a mess or something?" Shane's voice was teasing.

"No," he drew the word out on a laugh. "You're more than welcome to come by."

"Cool. I'll be there in a bit."

Shane hung up before Justin could say anything else. He dropped his phone beside him on the couch and kicked his feet up onto the coffee table while he waited.

3

W HEN SHANE woke up that morning, Justin had been the first thing he'd thought of. He had rolled from his nice, warm, lonely bed and walked to the kitchen. A stack of boxes and the baggies with the bushings in them were leaning against his sliding door. He noticed the time; the parts store had been open for a good half hour and had already delivered his order.

They're on it today.

He had walked back to his bedroom after he started the coffeemaker. Stretched out on the bed, he'd snagged his phone from the nightstand and scrolled through his list until he found Justin's number. The phone rang a few times until his voice mail picked up. He left a message then dropped his phone beside him on the bed.

Shane ended up drinking half a pot of coffee before he loaded his car and headed to Justin's place. The butterflies in his stomach reminded him of his younger years and crushing on the quiet guy who sat in the back of almost all of his high school classes.

.   .   .

It wasn't long before Shane was beating on his door. Justin went and let him in. He eyed the boxes in Shane's hands, curiosity killing him. Patience was *not* his middle name.

"Come on in. Make yourself at home." That was him, the ever-polite host. Wouldn't Mom be proud?

"Don't freak out, okay?"

"Huh? Why would I freak?" Justin frowned at him.

"I brought some stuff for you. It's a gift, but if it makes you feel better, you can work it off. But it's not required."

"What did you do?"

Shane stacked the boxes on the couch and topped off the pile with the clear pouches. He backed away with a wide grin on his face, a mixture of pride and anxiousness.

Justin moved cautiously toward them, shooting glances at Shane. His jaw dropped as he picked up the pouches. Door bushings with their pins for each hinge. The first box held speakers, and not cheap ones either. In the last box was a stereo with CD player and an iPod jack. He'd seen that stereo at the parts store. He'd drooled over it until he saw the price tag.

"I can't take this, Shane."

"Sure you can. I told you. You can work it off."

"I'll have to live at your garage to pay all this off!"

"There's no hurry. Look, man, I have an account at the store. It'll take weeks, if not months for you to save enough. Let me do this for you."

"Why? Why would you do this?" Justin asked. He still held the stereo. He couldn't make himself put it down.

"'Cause I wanted to. From one gearhead to another."

Justin stared at him for a long moment. Shane wasn't going to take no for an answer; Justin could see it on his face. Resignation fell over him like a warm blanket. Or maybe it was something else. Justin really wanted the parts, and it would be months before he could afford them on his own.

"I'll work off the cost of the stereo and speakers and take the door bushings as a gift." Justin nodded. After all, he did have some pride. He also had enough sense not to look a gift horse in the mouth.

"Deal."

"Thank you." Justin smiled at Shane and let himself get excited for the first time since Shane walked through his door.

"That's better." Shane grinned.

"What?" Justin asked.

"The smile on your face. It's in your eyes now."

Warmth spread through Justin's chest. His smile widened. "I'm happy. Hearing my own voice was getting old. I can't sing."

Shane laughed. Justin dropped down on the couch and opened the box in his hands. He knew he should put the bushings in his doors, but this stereo would go in first. He pulled out the instruction manual and started reading.

"I see how it is. I bring you presents, and now you're going to ignore me," Shane said, still laughing.

Justin laughed up at him. "I'm not ignoring you. I told you to make yourself at home."

"Yeah, yeah. I hear you."

Justin watched Shane walk into the kitchen. He heard the fridge door open and close, then various cupboards. A few minutes later, the coffee pot came to life. Justin didn't use the thing much, but Mom had gotten it for him for

Christmas one year, so he kept it. In case anyone came over and wanted some, he kept a small container of coffee in the cupboard. Justin had no idea if it was a decent brand, but the lady he'd asked at the corner store said it would do.

"How late you working tonight?" Shane asked from beside Justin.

"I get off at nine."

"Come over after you get done, and I'll help you put your stereo in. Then I'll throw a couple steaks on the grill."

"Cool. What should I bring?"

"Yourself, the stereo and the speakers. You can grab stuff to make salad if you want."

"You got it."

Shane was very alpha. He expected his directions to be followed. It was becoming increasingly obvious that arguing with him would be a waste of time. Justin didn't really mind. Living alone, being single, he made his own decisions all the time.

AFTER WORK, JUSTIN CHANGED INTO JEANS AND A T-shirt in the men's restroom. He didn't want to spend the evening in his gross uniform like the night at Denny's. He sprayed on some cologne to mask the stale grease smell and then left. After a quick stop at the grocery store, he headed for Shane's, ten minutes away.

He spotted Shane's car parked in front when he reached the house, leaving the driveway open for him to whip into. Smoke rose from the back of the house. As soon as Justin shut off his car and stepped out, he could smell the meat on the grill. His mouth watered; it wasn't often he had steak, and he looked forward to this one. He reached into his car and pulled the bag of salad fixings from the seat.

Justin walked around the house and found Shane manning the grill in a white T-shirt stretched tight across his muscles, and a pair of tight-fitting jeans. All six foot of him, with tongs in one hand and a beer in the other, stood there looking like a bad boy model for Wrangler or Budweiser.

Lord have mercy.

Justin cleared the interest from his face before Shane turned to see him coming. He gave Shane a nod and a smile and moved toward him. Shane returned Justin's smile and looked back down at the task in front of him.

"Help yourself to anything you need in there." Shane jerked his head toward the sliding glass doors on the back of the house. "How do you like your steak?"

"Medium. A little pink in the middle is cool with me," Justin answered, walking toward the door. "I brought two different dressings. I wasn't sure what you liked."

"Me? I'll eat anything that doesn't eat me first." Shane rubbed his hand over his gut, drawing Justin's eyes and making his mouth water again.

Visions of all sorts of eating invaded his thoughts. Justin turned abruptly away and went into the house. Thinking about his mouth on Shane had his temperature rising. He needed to cool off before embarrassing himself. Justin busied himself with throwing the salad together. The bowls and utensils were fairly easy to find. He managed to dice the tomato without cutting off a finger and sprinkled cheese across the top. He started to clean up his mess while he hid in the kitchen.

Shane tapped on the glass door and held up the plate of steaks. Justin couldn't hide anymore. He balanced the salad and dressing bottles and went back outside. The picnic table sat between the grill and house. Styrofoam plates and bottles of Pepsi lay on top, along with real forks and knives. Justin put the salad bowl beside the meat and took a seat on one side.

Shane sat down across from him and reached for his soda. He cracked open the top and nodded at the steaks. "Take one. Doesn't matter which."

"They look great." Justin stabbed the one on top and moved it to the plate in front of him. "I could smell them as soon as I got outta my car."

"Thanks. Don't expect gourmet here, but I can grill," Shane said with a grin.

4

DISHES WASHED and put away, they stood beside the garage door. The new stereo and speakers were vibrating the driveway. Oh, wait. That was him bouncing on the balls of his feet. After dinner, they'd gone straight to the garage and started tearing into Justin's car. He took the dash apart, and Shane had done the wiring. That wasn't something Justin did often enough, so Shane had taken care of it. While he did the wiring, Justin cleaned up from dinner. Shane's kitchen sparkled, everything in its place.

It was near midnight, and Shane had neighbors, so they didn't have the music cranked. With the windows down and the car parked close by, they could hear it clearly, though.

"Thank you." Justin grinned.

"Now you won't have to hear yourself singing." Shane laughed.

"Heck yeah. That sounds awesome!"

"You'll have to set your own channels, but the clock is done. I left the equalizer at the defaults, so you might need to adjust those as well."

"I'll listen to anything as long as it isn't me," Justin joked.

"You wanna come inside for a beer?" Shane asked.

"Sure. I'm too excited to go home to bed."

"Excellent." Shane walked to the car and turned off the ignition. He tossed the keys Justin's way, and Justin dropped them into his pocket. He followed Shane into the house and stood near the sink while Shane headed for the fridge. Justin saw him look around. "Damn. I don't think my kitchen has ever been this clean."

"I put everything back where I found it," he told Shane, for something to say. Compliments weirded him out. Justin didn't think he'd done anything worthy. Shane did most of the hard work—grilling steaks and installing Justin's stereo. Justin made a salad. The least he could do was clean up.

"I wasn't too worried about it. I'd find it eventually." Shane had their beers in his hand as he rounded the center island and moved toward the table. He sat down at the head and opened both bottles. Justin followed and sat down in the chair next to his.

"So, you seeing anybody?" Shane asked.

"Not really," Justin hedged.

"What does that mean?"

"Why do you want to know?" Justin asked.

"I never see you with anyone, so I was curious." Shane shrugged, lifting the bottle to his lips and taking a long pull.

"Nah." Justin shook his head and started peeling the label on his bottle.

"Yeah, me either," Shane said.

Silence fell over the table.

"What do you do when you're not working or fixing up your car?" Shane asked.

"I read. Or I sleep." He took a healthy drink and set the

bottle back on the table. "Not exactly the life of the party."

"What do you read?" Shane asked.

"Car manuals and how-to books, mostly," Justin said. "That's how I learned most of what I've done to my car."

"You learned that from a book?" Shane looked truly surprised by that.

"Yeah...."

"You should go to school. If you can do that well from a book, school should be no problem."

"I'm saving up. I'd like to go someday. But not for working on my ride. That I do for fun and because I love that car," Justin said.

"What do you want to go to school for?" Shane's tone was curious.

"I want to be a counselor for teenagers." Justin ducked his head.

"What kind of counselor?"

"Someday, I'd like to open a youth center. Shit costs so much; both parents have to work, so a lot of teenagers spend too much time alone. I mean, there's the jocks involved in one sport or another and the band kids who have practice. What do the other kids have to do? I could have a place with a library and computers and a gym." The longer Justin talked, the more excited he became. "Some of those kids don't have an adult they can count on. I want to make a difference."

"I'm impressed." Shane nodded. "Hey. What if you had a garage too? Teenagers should know how to work on their vehicles, at least to change the oil and tell when something is wrong. I would be willing to lend some time, teaching them."

Justin laughed.

"What's so funny?" Shane looked offended.

"I haven't even started school and you're volunteering to teach at the youth center I don't have."

Shane seemed to think about it for a minute, then shook his head. He chuckled and finished off his beer. "I guess I did get ahead of myself, didn't I?"

"Maybe a little."

Shane stood and picked up his empty bottle. "You want another?"

"I haven't finished this one yet." Justin raised his bottle to take a swallow while Shane walked away to get himself another. He ogled Shane's ass from the corner of his eye. *Damn.* He took a longer drink and realized he'd finished his beer too. Justin stood up to throw the bottle away.

"I thought you weren't empty," Shane said.

"I didn't have as much left as I thought."

Shane reached into the fridge and grabbed a second bottle. Justin was straightening from closing the cupboard when he turned to find Shane standing in front of him. He swallowed and forced a casual smile.

"You surprise me at every turn, you know that?" Shane said roughly.

"How do you mean?"

"You aren't what I was expecting."

"What were you expecting?" Justin asked quietly.

"Not this."

Shane set the bottles on the counter and stood with his feet spread. He was watching Justin and looked like he was wrestling with something. If Justin hadn't been sure he was projecting, he'd have sworn Shane was thinking of kissing him. But that couldn't be right. Guys like Shane didn't go for guys like him. They had chicks falling all over them, a different one every weekend. They weren't gay like him.

Justin's heart pounded, and his stomach dropped to his feet. He wasn't ready for this. *I like him.* Shane wasn't just sexy, he was nice, and Justin could see this going south. "I have to go," he whispered.

"You do?" Shane asked. His look changed to confusion.

"Yeah. I have a thing in the morning," Justin said.

"What kind of thing?" Shane wanted to know.

"I, uh, a work thing," Justin lied. He didn't give Shane time to say anything else. "Thanks for dinner and putting my stereo in. I'll see ya later." He bolted, like the chicken he was.

When Justin pulled out of the driveway, he saw the silhouette of Shane in the window, watching him go.

WHAT THE HELL WAS THAT ALL ABOUT?

Shane replayed the last five minutes in his head as he walked to the window. He didn't need to peel the thin, white curtain back to watch Justin drive away. The streetlight across the road provided plenty of light.

He was 99 percent sure Justin had lied about having a work thing the next day. The flash of fear in Justin's eyes right before he bailed told Shane something had freaked him out. He'd grabbed another beer from the fridge and turned around to find Justin standing behind him. The excitement of his new stereo still bright in Justin's eyes and the damp shine of his lips had Shane staring. He'd wanted to kiss those lips, see if he could make Justin's eyes change color with need. Shane had fought himself; he didn't want to scare Justin away by doing something stupid. Had Justin seen the war going on inside Shane? Was that what drove him away? Possibly. Shane should apologize, but he didn't feel sorry.

5

JUSTIN AVOIDED Shane, even volunteered for extra shifts, assuming Shane wouldn't make a scene at his job. He didn't. Oh, Shane had come by, but Justin hid in the back. After Shane called his phone and texted with no response, he quit trying there. Justin even went grocery shopping in an effort to not be home if Shane showed up.

On the third day of no contact, Justin came home to find Shane parked in front of his house. The tight set of Shane's lips showed his displeasure at Justin's cowardice. The reasons Justin gave himself sounded lame even to him. He wondered what Shane would say about them. Justin parked his car and headed for the front door. Behind him, he heard the slam of a car door, and he knew Shane was coming. After he unlocked the door, Justin walked inside and left the door hanging open. Neither of them had spoken yet and dread was coiling in Justin's stomach at the words Shane would say.

The quiet click of the front door closing had him glancing over his shoulder. But he kept walking into the kitchen. Justin opened the fridge, reached inside, and pulled two bottles of soda from the shelf.

When he turned around, Shane was standing right in front of him. Shane's arms were crossed over his chest, and the muscles in his clenched jaw were ticking.

"You're avoiding me, and I want to know why," Shane said.

"I've been busy, working," Justin replied.

"That's a bunch of bull and you know it." Shane leaned forward. "I don't do lies. That will piss me off faster than anything else."

"Sorry...," Justin mumbled.

Shane crowded Justin against the counter, and Justin couldn't tear his eyes away from him. Justin's breath was coming in short bursts while his heart tattooed excitement against his ribcage. He could have slid left or right as his arms fell to his sides, but moving out of Shane's path was the last thing Justin wanted to do. He licked his parted lips and watched Shane's eyes drop to his mouth before returning to search Justin's eyes. What was he looking for? More importantly, what was he waiting for? If Shane didn't kiss him in the next ten seconds, Justin would lose his mind for sure.

Shane lifted his hand and laid it against Justin's neck. Slowly, he moved it up Justin's neck to brace his jaw. He leaned in and growled. "Tell me to walk away."

"I—I can't." Justin breathed.

Shane dove in and pressed his lips to Justin's. He wasn't gentle. Justin didn't want him to be. His breath caught and the soda bottles fell, forgotten, to the counter. He braced his hands on the counter behind him and let his eyes close. Shane tilted his head and pressed his mouth harder to

Justin's, forcing his lips apart. He sucked Justin's bottom lip between his, nipped it, and moved to his upper lip.

Justin raised his hands from the counter to grip Shane's muscled shoulders. A shiver slid through Shane, and he moved closer. Justin could feel the hard planes of his chest under the palms of his hands.

God, what I wouldn't give to feel his bare skin instead of the soft cotton of his shirt.

Shane flexed the hand at Jason's neck, and the pressure of his mouth on Justin's tilted Justin's head back. He moaned with Shane's handling of him. He pushed his tongue into Justin's mouth to slide against his. Justin's fingertips dug into Shane's shoulders.

Shane moved his hand from Justin's neck and put both of his hands on Justin's hips. He lifted Justin as if he weighed nothing and sat him on the edge of the counter. Shane pressed his body between Justin's knees, and Justin whimpered, freaking whimpered, when Shane's crotch brushed against his. He lifted his feet to hook around Shane's ass. As Shane's hard length pressed against his, Justin's feet flexed to pull him closer. Justin curled his fingers in the fabric at his shoulders. The tip of Shane's tongue licked the roof of Justin's mouth. It tickled, sending delicious shivers down Justin's spine.

Shane pulled back, licking his swollen lips and breathing hard. "Now. Why were you avoiding me?"

"I like you," Justin said.

"I like you too. Obviously."

The way he said it, Justin heard the confusion in Shane's voice.

How do I explain?

"No. I like you. You, you're straight?" Justin's brain function had started to work again, and now he was the confused one. "But you kissed me, so you can't be straight."

"I'm pretty sure you were a full participant in that kiss." Shane gave him a half grin and jerked his head to where Justin's hands were still holding on to his shirt. "No, I'm gay. I just don't advertise it."

"I've seen gorgeous girls hanging all over you."

"Friends. For show. It keeps other women from bothering me."

"Oh."

"So you thought those were girlfriends? And because I was straight, I'd reject your friendship because you aren't?"

"Kind of. More like my having other-than-friend feelings for you would weird you out. I was trying to avoid an awkward situation."

"I see. And now?"

"I'm still processing." Justin's hands took on a mind of their own, releasing Shane's shirt and starting the journey over his wide chest. His eyes were locked on Shane's as he explored. His eyebrow rose with the caress of his palms.

"Processing? They used to call this making out, but it's been a while."

"I think there's more kissing involved in making out."

Shane chuckled, and Justin felt the rumble under his hands. "If you're hinting for another kiss, I could possibly help you out."

"Shhhh. I'm concentrating," Justin said.

Shane didn't say anything. He leaned in to run his nose against Justin's temple, down to his ear and then down his neck. His lips pressed against the skin there and traveled across Justin's shoulder. Justin could feel the heat of Shane's breath through his shirt, and he gave up his exploration and pushed at Shane's chest. Shane lifted his head and leaned back, giving him a questioning look. Justin didn't play the aggressor very often. Okay, never. He sat on his ass and waited for the other guy to make the move.

"What's wrong?" Shane asked.

Justin took a deep breath and let it out slowly. "I want to kiss you."

"Okay. And that put that look on your face, why?"

"Because I rarely ask for anything. I didn't know how to ask or what to do." Justin looked down at the floor.

"Justin. Look at me."

He raised his head, slowly, worrying his lip between his teeth.

"You want something from me, you ask for it. Just say it, straight up. I don't like guessing games, and I'm not a mind reader. You might have noticed that I don't ask. I like having my way, and I might be stubborn at times, but what you want or need is no less important."

"It's never been before...," Justin said quietly. He raised his voice. "Kiss me. Please."

Shane moved his hands up Justin's back, pulling him closer. The moment their lips touched, Justin sighed. This was what he wanted, had been wanting since the dinner at Denny's. He tilted his head and parted his lips, inviting Shane in for a taste. Shane took Justin's offer and slid his tongue against his. This kiss was slower, more sensual. Justin pulled Shane tighter against him as his motor hummed.

Shane pulled away and licked his lips. "As much as I'm enjoying this, we should slow it down. How 'bout a movie?"

Heat crept up Justin's neck to warm his face. "A movie. Yeah." He pushed Shane back until he could climb down from the counter. "Go ahead and pick something out. I'll make us some popcorn."

Shane strode into the next room with a confident swagger. Justin's eyes landed on the seat of his pants, after he watched the muscles under Shane's shirt flex with his movements.

Lord have mercy on my soul.

6

J USTIN SHOWED up the next morning with coffee and pastries, in crappy jeans and shirt, intent on helping Shane with whatever project he was working on. After they ate, they went outside to the garage and got to work. The Camaro in the driveway had blown its motor. They were tearing it down to put the new crate motor in. The owner knew what needed to be done, but he didn't have the time or knowledge to drop a new motor into his car. Shane's reputation stood out around town, so the guy had called and had it towed over.

"So. Next weekend the race track opens. You wanna go?" Shane said.

Shane had his head buried under the hood and his ass in the air. The shirt he wore had the sleeves ripped off to leave his arms bare. Justin was supposed to be helping, but mostly he stood and stared. Every ripple of Shane's muscles had Justin's mouth drying out.

"If I can get it off work, yeah," Justin said.

"Have you ever been?"

"Um, *no*."

Shane laughed and pulled himself to standing. A ten millimeter wrench spun around the end of his little finger. "You'll need earplugs or noise-dampening headphones. It gets really loud."

Justin nodded, excitement already starting to build inside him. "I'll grab something this week."

"Wear jeans and a T-shirt, but bring a sweatshirt for later. It'll probably be pretty late when we get home." Shane eyed him for a minute. "You could pack a bag and stay over here, if you want. I have a spare bedroom...."

Justin had the feeling if he stayed overnight at Shane's, the spare bedroom wouldn't be where he slept. "Thanks." He smiled.

"What?" Shane said.

"What 'what'?"

"You got a look when I said you could stay over."

"I didn't."

"You did." Shane growled. "What did I tell you about lying?"

"I don't think I'd be sleeping in the spare bedroom if I stayed. It made me nervous for a minute," Justin said.

"You don't have to be nervous. I won't push for something you aren't ready for. I'm not in a hurry."

"Why not?"

"Because I am really tired of coming home to nothing. If we're going to do this, really do this, I want to do it right."

"Thank you." Justin sighed and looked down at his shoes. "You've treated me better than anyone ever has, and I appreciate that."

"Don't thank me for not being an asshole. I have my moments of assholery. You'll see." Shane disappeared back under the hood of the Chevy. "Can you run in the house and grab us something to drink?"

"Sure." He hadn't been doing anything, anyway. Justin laid the pliers on the trunk lid and rounded the car, heading for the house.

Inside the kitchen, he walked to the fridge and threw open the door. The six-pack of soda on the shelf made him smile. Shane had picked up the brand Justin preferred, in the size he always bought. He pulled two bottles from inside and closed it up again. He tried to wipe the goofy grin off his face, but it wouldn't go away.

Justin fought the grin all the way out to the car and Shane, but he lost. "Here you go."

Shane pulled himself from under the car and turned to take the bottle. "What's the grin for?"

"You," Justin said.

"What did I do?" Shane didn't do innocent well.

"Kiss me," Justin blurted.

Shane's eyebrow winged up along with the corner of his mouth. "Because I stocked the fridge with soda for you?"

"It's kind of hard to explain," Justin said. He gripped the bottle, sliding his hands back and forth around it in the condensation.

Shane took Justin's bottle from his hands and set both bottles on the fender of the car. He gripped the front of Justin's shirt and pulled him closer until their breath mingled. Justin watched him tilt his head, and then Shane's tongue shot out to lick Justin's nose. Justin chuckled and closed the distance between them. The kiss was chaste, but lingered.

Justin leaned back, away from Shane, still smiling.

"Now, tell me why," Shane said.

"Everyone I've ever been with has treated me like a fuck toy. No one has ever noticed me, let alone what soda I drank."

"Well, they were stupid." Shane shrugged. He turned to pick up the bottles and handed Justin's to him. "Now, do you think you might do some work instead of standing there? As flattering as it is to have your eyes on my ass, it's also distracting."

A grin stretched across Justin's face. "Not my fault you've got a great ass," he mumbled. He went around the front of the car and picked up a screwdriver. He started in on the clamps holding the hoses in place. Shane had already drained the fluids from the car, before either of them attempted to take any parts off. Neon green antifreeze with bits of dirt trickled from the end of the first hose as he lifted his body from leaning over the fender. Justin turned to toss it toward the trash and caught Shane watching him. "What?"

"Nothing." Shane shook his head. "Just you being you."

"What'd I do?"

"You're getting more comfortable with me."

"Yeah. I am." He was. Shane forced him to own his confidence. Little by little his protective shell was cracking like a cicada shedding its exoskeleton. He laughed at the thought.

"Wanna share?"

Justin shook his head. "Nah. Just a passing thought."

Shane shrugged. "Okay." He bent his head and went back to work.

Justin watched Shane between taking hoses off the motor. The concentration on Shane's face fascinated Justin, so it took longer than it should have to finish his task. "I'm done. What do you want me to start on next?"

Shane lifted his head and looked at the clock. "How 'bout we take a lunch break?"

Justin's stomach growled, and he laughed. "I could eat."

"You're always hungry," Shane teased.

"Pretty much." Justin wagged his brows at Shane and grinned. "You want me to run and get us something?"

"No. I have stuff in the fridge for sandwiches, and there's carrots and chips. We can sit on the picnic table if you want," he said.

"Sounds good to me. Even I can't screw up sandwiches."

7

T HE SUN wasn't even up when Shane pulled up in front of Justin's place on Saturday morning. Shane should have been tired. He'd been too keyed up to sleep well. The tall cup of coffee beside him would keep him awake until they got to the track. That and the man walking toward him. Shane leaned across the front seat, unlatched the door, and pushed it open.

Justin tossed his sweatshirt in the back and slid into his seat. He pulled the door shut behind him and turned to smile at Shane. The sleepy-eyed curve of his lips begged for a kiss. Shane poked a finger in the collar of his shirt and tugged him closer. Their warm breath mingled before the first brush of his lips. The kiss started lazy, slow until his mouth persuaded Justin's to open. His tongue swept inside, tasting toothpaste and the unique flavor of the man in his arms. Justin moaned, and Shane echoed the sound.

"Good morning," Shane said when he pulled back.

"Mmm... good morning to you too," Justin said.

Shane smiled. "You ready for this?"

"Yeah. I've been looking forward to this all week."

Putting the car in gear, Shane agreed. He pressed down on the accelerator and roared down the road. "You're gonna have a blast!"

The drive to the track would take a couple of hours. Shane reached over and took Justin's hand in his. "How was work last night? Were you busy?"

"It was steady, right up till I left." Justin shifted his hand so he could weave his fingers between Shane's. "I couldn't wait for the night to be over. Did you make any progress on that motor?"

"I finished it about midnight. It would have been done three days ago if the parts I needed hadn't been on backorder," Shane said.

"Mr. Reynolds will be happy. How's it sound?"

Is he serious? Shane's eyebrows shot up, and he glanced at Justin before focusing back on the road. "Excuse me?"

Justin coughed, choked, then started laughing. He laughed so hard, the only thing keeping him from doubling over was the seat belt across his chest. Shane had never seen him laugh like that. Did Justin even realize the way his eyes danced when he laughed from deep inside? Shane noticed. He wanted to press his mouth to Justin's and drink the laugh from his lips to keep it safe. Too bad he was driving.

An hour later, Justin was sacked out with his head leaning against the window and his relaxed fingers still entwined with Shane's. Shane kept the music turned down while he drove so it wouldn't wake his date. A few times since Justin had fallen asleep, the excitement inside Shane weighed his foot on the accelerator until they were way past speeding. He'd backed off... a little.

I can't wait to see his face when the first car blows by him.

The line of cars ahead of him caused him to slow down, and he waited his turn. He tightened his fingers around Justin's and gave an easy tug. "Hey. Babe. Wake up."

"I fell asleep." Justin yawned, straightening in his seat.

"I wondered why it got so quiet," Shane teased.

"Sorry."

"Nothing to be sorry for." Shane shot a grin over at him. "We're here."

Justin took in the line of cars before them and leaned left and then right. "I hope the line moves fast. I wanna go inside."

"Same here. You're gonna love this." He couldn't help the pride filling him. Justin would enjoy himself, and Shane would be the one giving him the experience.

THE LINE MOVED SLOW AND STEADY, SO THE WAIT wasn't ridiculous. When Justin saw the number of people walking from the parking lot and inside the track grounds, he was amazed they hadn't waited longer. He looked around from the inside of the car, taking in everything while Shane parked and shut off the engine. He leaned across the seat in his excitement and stole a quick, chaste kiss from Shane. The surprise on Shane's face made him grin from ear to ear. "Come on. Let's go!"

"Uh, yeah, okay." Shane opened his door and stood up. He turned and reached into the backseat for a pair of ear plugs joined by a string so he could wear them around his neck.

Justin grabbed his headphones in one hand and his bottle of soda in the other. They met at the back of the car, both wearing excited grins. "Let's head in."

"I'm following you," Justin said.

Shane walked through the parking area with Justin beside him. Justin put his headphones around his neck to free up one hand. *Would it weird Shane out if I reached for his hand?* For the time being, he'd play it cool and resist. At least until the daylight waned.

The track was massive inside the gate. It had looked huge from outside, but once they could see the midway, Justin could see a mile of people of every age, shape, and size milling about. Tents of various colors and logos lined both sides. Tables held parts, pamphlets, and memorabilia. At one end of the stands, food vendors were set up around the souvenir shop and restrooms, with porta-potties on the other end of the grandstand.

"Awesome, isn't it?" Shane said, watching Justin's face.

"It's fantastic."

"Wanna walk down through? I'd like to show you something."

"Sure," Justin said, smiling and still looking around.

"My uncle brought me here the first time when I was about ten. I knew when I left, cars were my future," Shane said.

They stopped behind a tractor-trailer with a name on the side that Justin had never heard of. An awning spread from the top edge of one side to hook on poles. Underneath was a handful of men surrounding a motor. They worked feverishly, assembling it as Justin and Shane watched. Minutes passed, and the men were hooking up the engine to a machine and firing it up. Justin was fascinated.

"Cool, isn't it?" Shane said. "C'mon. Let's keep moving,"

"Okay," he took in the action one more time before turning away to follow. "How soon will the racing start?"

Shane glanced at his watch. "The street cars are going now. The big ones, in a few minutes. Let's head over and find a place to stand."

They wound their way through the crowd and between the bleachers to find an open spot along the fence. Everyday cars of every style, make, and model flew down the track in pairs.

"When the nitro cars come out, you'll want your headphones," Shane said after Justin took his fingers out of his ears.

He looked over his shoulder, smiling. "Okay."

"Look." Shane pointed to the track starting line.

The nitro cars were lining up behind the announcer's booth. Justin gripped the top of the fence and leaned forward for a better look. He could hear the rumble of their motors clear down the track where they stood.

8

AFTER THE last pair of street cars took the track, the announcers started talking about the main event. When they finished, Shane and Justin put on their headphones and watched the first pair of funny cars do burnouts on the track. Shane's attention was divided between the cars and watching Justin's face. Justin's excitement was contagious, not that Shane wasn't already wound up. He lived for summer and going to the track. Unfortunately the track close to home had only two major events. One was at the end of June and the other at the beginning of August. Until he had someone to share racing with who would appreciate it as much as he did, Shane didn't spend the money or time traveling to any other tracks. If Justin had as good a time as he expected, that could change.

Justin's whoop and the way he practically bounced in place at the first pass, Shane knew he was hooked. His own smile broadened. Wait until Justin saw the cars race after dark.

Shane felt a tug at his shirt and looked down. A boy,

probably five or six years old, smiled up at him. He smiled back at the boy. "Do you need something?"

"Can I stand here with you? My mommy said I had to ask," the boy said.

Looking back over his shoulder, Shane saw a young woman watching the boy and rubbing her hands over a very rounded stomach. He nodded to her with a smile and looked back down at the boy. "You sure can." Shane took a step back and pointed to the spot in front of him. "You can stand here."

"Thank you!" The boy beamed as he gripped the fence in front of him.

"Is this your first time?" Justin asked the boy. "It's my first time."

"Oh no. This is my second! I'm going to come every week until my little sister gets here, and then we'll bring her too!"

"What's your favorite part?" Justin asked.

"I like the burnouts best!"

Shane chuckled and nodded. "Those are pretty awesome. Do you know what that light is called?" Shane pointed to the head of the track.

The boy snorted and rolled his eyes. "Everyone knows that's the Christmas tree. That's what tells the drivers when to go."

"Oh, you're a smart one," Shane said.

The boy went back to his mother after the last pair of cars ran. She thanked Shane and Justin for letting her son hang out with them before leading him away for a restroom break.

At a lull in the action, Shane and Justin left their spot at the fence to find food. The lines for the restrooms and food were the longest they'd been all day, but Shane didn't mind the wait. Justin hadn't stopped smiling in so long Shane wondered if his face hurt.

"What are you hungry for?" Shane asked. "I'll probably just get a dog. Maybe some fries."

"Sounds like a plan to me," Justin agreed.

They stood in line for several minutes until it finally became their turn, then ordered and got out of the way for the next customer. After the worker handed them their food, they walked away from the crowd to find a place to eat in peace.

Later when the sun went down, they found seats in the bleachers. Shane thought Justin was going to flip when the first funny car blew past.

"Did you see how high the flames were?"

"Pretty cool, huh?" Shane grinned.

Between rounds, they wandered through the booths and stopped to watch crews work on their cars. Shane offered to get Justin an autograph or two, but he declined. "Maybe next time," he said. That was good. Justin was talking about a next time.

It was late when the last pair made its run. Shane and Justin wove through the crowd to get back to their car and head home. Shane didn't figure Justin would sleep on the way home with the way he still grinned.

"Are you staying over tonight or do you want me to drop you at your place?" Shane wanted to know, in case he was wrong and Justin did pass out. After all, the man hadn't gotten much sleep the night before, and sooner or later it would catch up with him.

"Whichever is easiest for you," Justin answered.

"Either is fine with me. I don't have to be up early. Do you?"

"Not real early, no. I have to work tomorrow, well, later tonight." It was after midnight.

"You can just stay over, and I'll fix you breakfast in the morning before I take you home," Shane decided. He was looking forward to it, actually.

"I like steak and eggs, homemade biscuits, and it all served in bed, my good man." Justin spoke with a fake aristocratic accent.

"Yes, sir, Justin, sir. Is there anything else I can do for you? Mint on your pillow? Tuck you in? Perhaps you'd like a bedtime story?" Shane said.

"*Yes.* A bedtime story, but nothing too scary." Justin grinned.

"I'll see what I can do." Shane laughed, shaking his head.

Justin couldn't remember the last time he'd had so much fun. He watched Shane out of the corner of his eye as they headed home. Since he'd slept on the way up, he checked out his surroundings on the way back.

They passed farmland and drove through small towns you would miss if you blinked, but the best scenery Justin saw was Shane. With the road dark, he could watch Shane without being caught staring.

Since leaving the track, Shane had gone quiet. Justin wondered for a moment if he'd done something wrong but pushed the thought away as quickly as it came. They'd had a great day.

"Do you need both hands for driving?" Justin's heart thumped once at his out-of-the-blue question. *No, Shane told me if I wanted something to ask.*

"Not right now, I don't." Shane stuck his hand out to Justin.

"Just tell me if and when you need your hand back," Justin said as he clasped Shane's hand in his.

"I will." Shane turned his head to smile. "You're not sleepy?"

"I'm too keyed up to sleep. When do you think we can go back?" Justin saw Shane's smile widen in the glow of oncoming headlights.

"They have smaller events every few months during the summer. We'll have to look and see if there's anything coming up soon that we can do in a weekend. Can you get a weekend off?"

"Sure, as long as I ask a couple weeks in advance," Justin said.

"Great. When we get up in the morning, we'll go online and see what we can find," Shane said.

"Sounds good to me. So...."

"So...?"

"Do you like to dance?" Justin asked.

"Sure. I'm not very good at it, though," Shane said.

"Can you sway back and forth? Shake your ass?" Justin bit his lip to keep from laughing out loud.

"It so happens I can do both of those." Shane laughed.

"Sold! Would you like to go out with me Friday night? I'll buy you dinner, and then we can go have a beer somewhere there's a band playing," Justin said.

"Is this a date?" Shane asked, glancing at Justin with his brows drawn down.

"Uh.... Um.... Ah...."

"Justin, I'm kidding," Shane said. "Of course I'd love to go. Dress?"

"If you want, you can wear a dress. Didn't know you were into that. Interesting." Justin couldn't hold back the laugh this time.

"You'd be surprised what I'm into, little man." Shane didn't laugh.

"Oh, now you have to tell me. What secrets do you have, Mister?" Justin shifted in his seat so he could face Shane more without having to turn his head.

"If you want to play truth or dare, you have to wait until we get home," Shane grinned.

9

S HANE PULLED into his driveway and killed the engine. The ride home had been every bit as fun as the day spent at the track. Justin was starting to come out of his shell, revealing a great sense of humor. "I made up the guest room, in case you decided to stay." He'd like Justin to sleep in his bed, but he didn't want Justin to feel pressured.

"Thanks. That was nice of you," Justin said.

Was there something in Justin's tone, or was he imagining it? "You can sleep in my bed. I wouldn't object, but I can't promise you there won't be a hard-on against your ass in the morning." *There. Straight to the point.*

Justin climbed from the car without a word. Shane got out and rounded the car to stand in front of him. "What are you thinking? Sometimes it's hard to tell."

He looked into Justin's eyes as Justin seemed to think over his answer. "There are a lot of things going through my head right now. At first, I was sure you didn't want me in your bed, but I talked myself out of that one."

"Good. What else?"

"I want to sleep in bed with you, but I don't want this, us, to be like every other 'relationship'"—Shane could almost see the quotes around the mocking word—"I've had."

"How about this? Rules are, cuddling is okay. Bottom halves are clothed. No sex." Shane reached up with his right hand to run his knuckles along Justin's cheek. "Sex will happen, but not tonight." He leaned in to give Justin a chaste but lingering peck on the lips. "Deal?"

Justin licked his lips and smiled. "Deal."

They grabbed their stuff from Shane's car and went into the house. The clock read three o'clock. "Breakfast is probably going to be lunch. Let's get ready for bed."

"I'll change in your bathroom. Two minutes and I'll be ready," Justin said.

Stretching his arms over his head, Shane grunted and smiled. "I'll meet you in the hallway after I get outta these jeans."

Shane checked out Justin's ass as he walked away. How was he going to keep his hands to himself with that man in his bed? Maybe he should buy a chastity belt. The more time he spent with Justin, the more attracted he became. It wasn't just the sexy shape of Justin's body. It was the whole package.

Quit fucking off and get changed, idiot. Shane broke out of his daze and headed for his bedroom. A clean pair of sweatpants lay on the top of the basket of laundry he'd been meaning to fold.

Shit. He'll think I'm a slob.

Shrugging, Shane changed his clothes. Too late to worry about it now. He shoved the basket into a corner and went to meet Justin in the hallway. His timing was perfect. Justin stepped out of the bathroom wearing black sweats and a tank.

Rules, what rules? I want to get him naked now.

It was the outline of the nipple rings that did it. Shane's jaw clenched with the need to tug on them with his teeth. But he'd promised, and he had to keep being a man of his word if he wanted Justin to trust him. Thank God, his dick wasn't at full mast. That shit was hard to hide in sweats.

"Right this way, roomie." Shane swept his arm toward the open door of his bedroom. "Your pillow awaits."

It was going to be a long night....

"Are you always like this when you're tired?" Justin laughed and walked into the bedroom. He put his bag against the wall by Shane's dresser. The room was a deep green with beige carpet. It was neat, other than the overflowing basket of laundry in the corner. Even the bed was made.

"I'm not that tired, actually," Shane said.

"I like your room," Justin said. His own bedroom was a boring beige with boring brown carpet. The only color was the car pictures he had hung up.

"Thanks. It took me a while to decide on the colors. When I bought this place, the room was Pepto pink with dark pink carpet." He shuddered.

"Ewww." Justin tilted his head back and forth while staring at Shane. He couldn't picture the bald, muscular mechanic in a pink bedroom. "Yeah, I can't picture it."

Shane laughed. "Get in bed, man. You have to work later."

"Are you still wide awake?" Justin asked as he climbed into bed.

"Kinda. Why? Are you?" Shane climbed in on the opposite side.

"A little. Lay down on your stomach for me, would you?" Justin said. A split second decision had him flexing his fingers.

"What are you going to do to me?" But Shane did as he was asked.

"Torture you, of course," Justin said.

Shane jumped when Justin wrapped his cold hands on his shoulders. Justin cracked up. He couldn't help it. Seeing the big man flinch tickled him.

"Not funny," Shane grumbled.

"Was too," Justin said as he started to knead the muscles under his hands.

"Mmmm, are you trying to put me to sleep?" Shane groaned. "I didn't realize how tight my back was."

"Maybe, or maybe I just wanted an excuse to put my hands on you without breaking any rules." Justin grinned, though Shane couldn't see him.

"I like the way you think," Shane half laughed, half groaned.

Justin dug his fingers into Shane's back and continued his massage. He prayed his cock would behave, even as his heart beat faster. Shane closed his eyes, so Justin assumed he was drifting off. Smiling at his ability to make his boyfriend relax —was Shane his boyfriend? He couldn't think of another word to describe what they were to each other—Justin eased his hands until they were only running over Shane's firm back. *I'm taking total advantage.*

As the thought distracted him, he failed to notice Shane's

eyes open. One minute he was above Shane, the next under him. Justin looked up into Shane's burning eyes. "Uh...."

"Shhhh...," Shane whispered. He dropped his head to fuse their mouths together.

Justin moaned and opened his mouth to dance his tongue with Shane's. So much for hoping his dick would stay down. He could feel Shane's against his leg and knew he wasn't the only one affected.

Shane shifted until he was covering Justin from mouth to groin. When he started to rock, Justin's eyes crossed under his closed lids. He wrapped his arms around Shane's chest and curled his fingers into his shirt. His hips took on a mind of their own, lifting in time to Shane's rocking. When Shane leaned to the side and tugged his nipple ring through his shirt, Justin gasped. A shiver ran up his spine. He was about two seconds away from coming in his pants like a teenage virgin, but he wasn't interested in stopping.

Pulling his mouth away, Justin gulped air. His heart was hammering so hard in his chest a heart attack was a real possibility. "Shane...," he gasped.

"I'm not very good at following rules," Shane said as he continued to tug at Justin's nipple ring. He ground his hips in a circle, creating more friction with their dicks.

"Noticed.... Punish you later.... Make me come now," Justin said. He forced his eyes open to look up at Shane's face. There was lust there, but more. A hint of amusement too, but the affection Justin hoped he saw amazed him. It made the arousal he felt even more.

"Demanding...." Shane chuckled and then increased the tempo of his thrusts. His chuckle cut off abruptly with a groan.

Justin's eyes rolled back. "Yessss...." Grinding his teeth,

he tried to hold off as long as he could. He dug his heels into the mattress under him and pushed up, hard, as he lost control. "Oh God...."

"Justin...," Shane growled. He lowered his head and kissed Justin with more passion than Justin had ever felt from anyone else.

SHANE HAD PROMISED HIMSELF HE WAS JUST GOING TO lie there and enjoy the feel of Justin's hands on him. He couldn't remember the last time someone took the time to do for him, the way he did for other people. It was a nice change. And then Justin's hands had softened against him. The touch turned from soothing to sensual, and Shane's resolve had slipped away.

He'd only meant to go for a kiss, maybe a little groping. But the way Justin responded threw that out the window. One taste, one sound from Justin, and he wanted more. He wanted it all. Shane had promised no sex, though. He should have said "intercourse," because technically they'd just had sex with their clothes on. The sticky, cooling semen inside his pants proved that.

They should probably go clean up, but Shane couldn't stop kissing Justin. He'd never been one for kissing, except for foreplay, but he felt different with Justin. It was more than lust. It was respect and genuine affection.

Finally, when he couldn't stand it any longer, Shane pulled away from Justin. "We should go clean up."

"I, uh, don't have any other clothes except my jeans." Justin wore a satisfied look and a silly grin.

"I have some shorts you can wear. You'll have to tighten the drawstring, though, 'cause they'll be big on you." Shane rolled from the bed and walked to the dresser. He pulled out a pair of shorts and held them out to Justin while he climbed from the bed.

Justin wobbled a little before righting himself. Shane's ego swelled with the knowledge he'd made Justin's legs weak. A grin spread across his face. "Need help?" he asked, innocently.

Justin tossed him a look and shook his head. "I got it."

Shane chuckled. "Okay."

"Ass," Justin mumbled.

Shane burst out laughing. "I told you, I'm not good at following rules."

"Well, you don't have to look so proud of yourself," Justin said before leaving the bedroom.

Shane continued to grin while he cleaned himself up. He slipped into bed and under the covers to wait for Justin. When Justin came back, he climbed into bed and curled right into Shane's side, with his head on Shane's chest. No hesitation, nothing. Shane could get used to this. Seriously.

"Good night, Shane. Thank you for today," Justin whispered into the dark.

"You're welcome. Good night, babe," Shane whispered back.

10

THE SUN brightened the room until Shane had to blink a few times to get his eyes to adjust. He was tangled in sheets and Justin, and he couldn't be happier. That is, if his bladder wasn't being so insistent on him getting out of bed. Easing away without waking Justin, Shane slipped out of bed, then headed for the bathroom.

After his piss and washing his hands and face, Shane checked the time. It was a little after noon. Justin needed to be at work in a couple of hours, but Shane wanted to feed him before he took Justin home. Shane padded down the hall and into the kitchen to check the fridge situation. He had a couple of minute steaks and leftover baked potatoes. Steak, fried potatoes, and eggs with toast would be a filling brunch.

Shane got busy preparing their meal while Justin slept in his bed.

I could forget food and go back to bed.... No, he's got to eat before he leaves.

It was a struggle to stay in the kitchen, and he slipped a few times to sneak down the hall and peek in the bedroom.

I'm acting like a silly teenager. Jesus.

That thought was enough to keep him from making any more trips down the hall. Table set, steaks keeping warm in the oven, Shane was just finishing the scrambled eggs when Justin shuffled in, rubbing the sleep from his eyes. "What are you doing out here?"

"Making us something to eat. Did you sleep well?" Shane asked.

"I did until my pillow moved," Justin said, smiling.

"Sorry. I wanted to make sure you ate before I took you home." Shane filled the two plates on the table with scrambled eggs and turned back to the stove. He pulled the steaks from the oven and set the small pan in the middle of the table.

"That was nice of you," Justin said, sitting down.

"Don't tell anyone. I'm a mechanic. I'm supposed to have a filthy mouth and no manners." Shane winked.

"Your secret is safe with me." Justin laughed.

"Sit. Dig in. Scrambled eggs aren't good when they get rubbery." Shane busied himself with the toaster. If he'd had more time, he might have done biscuits, but they were on a little bit of a deadline.

Justin sat down at one of the plates, salted and peppered his eggs, and began eating. "What will you do after I leave today?"

"I dunno. Maybe I'll go to the arcade or just hang here. I have a ton of laundry I should actually put away, in case you missed the basket in the corner of my bedroom." Shane took his seat and dug into his own food. "So, how close to going to school are you? Or is that too personal?"

"No, it's okay." Justin wiped his mouth on the folded paper towel at the side of his plate. "I should be able to start next summer. Between what I'm putting back each paycheck and my income tax return, it'll be enough to start."

"And how do you feel about that? Are you nervous, excited?" Shane pushed his empty plate farther onto the table and leaned back in his chair.

"Both, but mostly excited. It will make me one step closer to my goal," Justin said. He got up from the table and started gathering dishes.

"What are you doing?"

"I'm helping with cleanup," Justin said, matter of fact.

"You're the guest. Guests don't do cleanup." Shane frowned at him.

GUEST? JUSTIN DIDN'T KNOW HOW HE FELT ABOUT THAT word. It kind of made him feel more like a favored uncle, rather than a bed partner. "Guest or not, I'm going to help with dishes. You'll just have to deal," Justin said.

"Whoa, who are you, and what did you do with Justin?" Shane raised his eyebrows.

It was Justin's turn to frown. "Huh?"

"Usually you back down and let me have my way," Shane said.

The night before—or early this morning—changed things for Justin. Why the clothed sex made him feel on more even ground with Shane, he wasn't sure, but it did. "I guess I do, don't I?" Justin grinned.

"You don't have to look so damn proud of yourself." Shane laughed and stood up from his chair to help clear the table.

"Sorry." He tried to wipe the grin from his face. The best he could do was smirk.

Justin wanted to stay on the assertive roll he was on and ask Shane to spend the night after their date Friday night, but the truth was, he was embarrassed for Shane to see his place. "So, Friday night? Are you going to be in disguise if I pick you up in my car?" He flashed a grin at Shane.

"Possibly. Do you have a fake mustache I can borrow?" Shane teased.

"Well, you did say you were wearing a dress. No one will probably recognize you in that. What color, do you think? I should match my shirt," Justin said.

"I knew it was too much to hope you forgot that part of the conversation." Shane shook his head. "Do you know I don't think I've ever been picked up for a date before?"

Justin stopped what he was doing and turned to face Shane. "Really?" A pang of sadness hit him in the chest. Shane was definitely the dominant in any relationship, but that didn't mean he shouldn't be taken care of too. Shane shrugged it off, but that didn't make Justin feel any better about it.

"C'mere," Shane said, emptying his hands.

Justin walked over to stand in front of him. "Yeah?"

Placing his hands on Justin's waist, Shane pulled him against his front. Justin didn't even have to think about it. He put his hands on Shane's shoulders and lifted up to kiss his lips. Shane smiled. "I have really enjoyed the last day and a half with you. Thank you for going yesterday and staying last night. Maybe next time, I'll let you finish the massage before I attack you. But that's a big maybe."

"Thank you for inviting me. I had a great time too," Justin said, smiling.

Shane sighed. "I know we aren't done with the dishes,

but we should get your things gathered up and head for your place. It's about that time...."

"I know, but I don't want the time to end," Justin whispered.

"This won't be the last time. Friday isn't that far away." Shane leaned down to capture Justin's mouth with his. The kiss was thorough, deep, and full of promise of things to come. When Shane lifted his head, Justin was weak in the knees, and they were both breathing hard. "C'mon before I decide to change my mind about letting you leave."

11

SHANE FINISHED his shower and dressed with time to spare. Justin wasn't due for a good half hour. The book he'd picked up earlier sat in a bag on the kitchen counter by the door so he wouldn't forget it. Maybe he was stepping on toes, maybe he wasn't. Everything was still so new between them. But Shane wanted to help.

He also had a duffel packed, in case Justin wanted him to stay over. Shane hadn't seen much of Justin's apartment the two times he'd been inside, only the living room and kitchen. It seemed a nice enough place, though. The right size for someone on his own.

Headlights came through the curtains as Justin pulled into his driveway. Shifting from one foot to the other, he'd wait for Justin to come to the door. This was a date, after all.

After Justin knocked, Shane picked up his two bags and then opened the door. "Hi." Shit. He was almost nervous.

"Hi." Justin smiled. "You look nice. Ready?"

"Thanks. You look good too. Where're you taking me?" Shane asked.

"A little place I know. It's usually not too crowded on Fridays. Now, Saturdays are a different story." He nodded toward the bags in Shane's hands. "What you got there?"

"Later. I'm hungry, and you promised to feed me."

Justin laughed. "That I did." He led the way to his car and walked around to the driver's side. "I've been excited about this all week."

Shane looked at Justin over the top of the car. "I have been too." It had truly been a long week, and he hadn't gotten to see Justin since Sunday when he'd dropped him off. They'd talked a couple of times on the phone, but one of them was either in the middle of something or about to go to bed. Not that Shane minded staying up late. Justin had been the one who insisted on cutting the calls short. If Shane couldn't see the excitement in Justin's face now, he might have been worried something was amiss. But no. They seemed to be all good.

They climbed into Justin's car. Before they could fasten seat belts, Shane leaned over to kiss Justin's lips. "Next time you pick me up for a date, that better be the first thing you do."

"I'm sorry, Master." Justin grinned.

"You don't look sorry," Shane said with his own grin.

"I guess we're even in the punishment department, then," Justin said.

Huh? "Punishment?" Shane asked. What in the world could he possibly have done to warrant punishment? *Oh.... Yeah.... Not following the rules in bed.* He couldn't stop his grin from widening. "I'll take that punishment anytime."

Justin laughed and shook his head. "You're incorrigible."

• • •

He hadn't been able to sit still all day. Minutes had ticked by like hours, only making him more anxious. This wasn't Justin's first date, but Shane was important to him, so he wanted the night to be perfect.

Sitting next to Shane in the car on the way to the little bar he knew, Justin still felt like he was going to crawl out of his skin. So many things were running through his brain. Would Shane like the food? Would he enjoy the music? What if it was more crowded than normal and they couldn't enjoy each other like a proper date?

"Did you get a lot accomplished this week?" Justin asked. The silence in the car wasn't helping his mood.

"I did. About half-a-dozen oil changes and tire rotations. I started rebuilding a motor Wednesday. If all my parts come in Monday, I should have it finished within a couple of days," Shane said. "How was work this week? Busy?"

"In spurts, it was. I spent a few hours rearranging the shelves in the back to try for more efficiency. We'll see how many complaints I get." Justin laughed. He worked with a lot of teenagers who didn't like to put more effort in than necessary. It was frustrating on a good day.

"I'm sure you'll get plenty, even if it needed to be done," Shane said.

Justin pulled into the parking lot and found a space. There was plenty to choose from. *Good. Doesn't look busy.*

"Have you ever been here before?" Justin asked.

"No. I've driven by a few times, though. Is this a hangout of yours?"

"Not really. I've been here a couple of times with people from work. Mostly, I've ordered food from here on my way home. My options are limited at midnight, and Denny's gets old," Justin said.

They got out of Justin's car and met at the front. *Awkward.* Justin wanted to hold Shane's hand, but they were in public. How would Shane feel about that? "It looks quiet. We shouldn't have any trouble finding a table or a seat at the bar," Justin said.

"Lead the way," Shane said.

12

USIC THUMPED from the jukebox speakers when they walked in. A few people were at the bar and a few at tables, but one side of the bar was vacant. They made their way over and slid onto two stools. Justin grabbed two menus then handed one to Shane.

Shane glanced between the menu in his hand and his surroundings. It definitely wasn't a sawdust-on-the-floor or Harleys-lined-up-out-front kind of place. It was dimly lit, classy, and neat as a pin.

"Can I get you two something to drink?" The bartender standing in front of them wore a white polo shirt and black dress pants. His hair was short and his mustache-goatee trimmed.

"I'll have a beer. Whatever you have on tap is fine," Shane said. He looked to Justin when he ordered the same. The bartender walked away with a nod.

"See anything on the menu you want?" Justin asked.

"I'm still deciding. How 'bout you?" Shane smiled.

"I'm thinking a steak salad." Justin folded his menu and stuck it back where he found it.

Shane looked down at his choices and decided on a chicken breast sandwich and fries. He opened his mouth to say something when the bartender came back with their beers.

"You don't recognize me, do you?" the bartender asked.

Shane frowned at him. "No, should I?"

"Lukas. Lukas Meed. We went to high school together," he said.

The name rang a bell, a whole choir of them. Back then, Shane had already been secure in his sexuality. He'd known Lukas was gay too, but they ran in different circles. Shane hung out with other grease monkeys while Lukas was an upper-class jock. They'd tried a relationship once, but it didn't work for long. There were too many obstacles in their way. Lukas sure looked different from the way he had back then. The long hair was gone. He'd grown into the bulky muscles he'd sported as a teen athlete. "Oh hey. How are you?"

"I'm great. How've you been?" Lukas asked.

"Good. Thanks for asking," Shane said. "So, you're bartending now?" *Obviously yes, if he was working behind the bar and serving their drinks. Good one, Shane.*

"Tonight, I am." Lukas smiled. "Someone called off last-minute, so the boss gets to pick up the slack."

"Boss? You're the manager, then?"

"Manager, owner, bartender, and occasional dishwasher." Lukas chuckled, then nodded toward Shane. "What are you doing these days?"

"I'm still turning wrench, only I own the garage." Shane smiled.

"Who's this?" Lukas jerked his head in Justin's direction.

"Oh, sorry. Lukas, this is Justin, a good friend of mine. Justin, Lukas and I went to high school together," Shane said.

"Nice to meet you. We're ready to order whenever you are," Justin said.

Shit. Shane had almost forgotten Justin was sitting there. Not good.

"Oh, sorry. Sure. What can I get you?" Lukas asked.

"I'll take a steak salad, extra ranch. Shane, what did you decide on?" Justin said.

There was something in Justin's tone Shane couldn't place. "Uh, the chicken sandwich and fries."

"I'll get your order in. Any appetizers?" Lukas glanced at Justin before focusing back on Shane.

"No, thank you," Justin said.

"Be right back."

Justin mumbled something that sounded like "Please don't."

"So.... Thanksgiving is coming. Will you go visit your mom?" Shane asked. What started out as a fun time had turned uncomfortable. *I'm ruining this.*

"Yeah. I'll stay with her and Dad Wednesday and Thursday and then come home Friday." Justin smiled. It was the first real smile he'd worn since their drinks arrived. "Do you have plans?"

"Dinner with my mom and working, probably. I'm not much for sitting still for long." Shane chuckled.

They were halfway through their beer and moving on to Christmas traditions when Lukas brought their dinners. "I'll bring you another drink. Let me know if you need anything else." As Shane opened his mouth to ask for ketchup, Lukas set a bottle in front of him.

"Thanks," Shane said.

"Yeah, thanks." Justin echoed.

13

"So, what are you two up to tonight?" Lukas asked. He reached back to his waist and pulled the rag from behind him to wipe the bar.

"Dinner and dancing," Shane said, winking at Justin.

"Sounds fun," Lukas said.

Justin was torn between getting up to leave, punching the bartender, or climbing into Shane's lap to stake his claim. He did none of those, sitting there like a bump on a log instead. Where was the confidence he'd finally started to feel with Shane? Justin couldn't seem to locate it, for the life of him. Sighing to himself, he picked at his salad. He was halfway through his second beer. Why couldn't he be one of those people who got bolder with a buzz? Then he could tell Lukas to go the hell away like he wanted. Justin pictured the way it would go....

"Don't you have other customers? My boyfriend and I are trying to enjoy our time together." Justin would give Lukas a pointed look.

Shane would look at him with surprise, and maybe he'd

be embarrassed by Justin's assertiveness. Though he did seem to like it when they were alone. Maybe Shane would wink at him again and show him some affection in front of Lukas. *That* would be great!

"Is there something wrong with your salad?" Lukas asked flatly.

"No, I'm just not as hungry as I thought," Justin answered, just as flatly.

Shane frowned but said nothing.

"Do you want me to box it up for you to take home?"

"Yeah, thanks," Justin said. Hurt warred with anger in his chest, yet he did nothing.

He'd been fooling himself to think he had a real chance with Shane. Lukas was a business owner, successful, and better looking. How could Justin compete, with his barely more than a minimum wage job and boring-ass apartment? He had hopes and goals, yeah, but Lukas was established.

This date was a disaster, and Justin couldn't wait for it to be over. So much for dancing the night away and ending it sleeping in Shane's arms.

When Lukas walked away with his untouched food, Shane turned to face him. "What's wrong?"

"I'm starting to not feel well." It wasn't a total lie. His stomach was in so many knots of dread, he thought he might be sick. Wouldn't that be the icing on the cake?

"Why didn't you say something? Let's go home," Shane said.

Lukas came back with the to-go box and the check. He handed both to Justin when he stuck his hand out for them. "Did I hear you say you're leaving? Already?"

"Justin's not feeling well, so yeah," Shane said, still frowning.

Justin pulled out his wallet and dug out his bank card to pay. Lukas took it over to run, and then wrote something on a piece of paper beside the machine. He was frowning himself when he came back. "I'm sorry. Your card wouldn't go through. No big deal, though. Sometimes it's good to be the boss. Dinner's on me, for the company."

Justin's face went hot, then cold as ice. *Impossible. I know there's money in my account.*

Lukas handed the card back to Justin and the piece of paper to Shane. "My number if you want to catch up again sometime."

"Thanks," Shane said, stuffing the paper into his pocket. He stood up, and Justin did too.

"Nice meeting you, Lukas," Justin said as he turned away and started for the door.

"You too, Jerry," Lukas called after him.

He couldn't even get my name right when he was ruining my life.

"Nice seeing you, Lukas," Shane said.

Shane followed Justin out and around to the driver's side of his car. "Are you okay to drive?"

"Yeah, it's not far," Justin said with a nod. *Please stop making me talk. I can only swallow so many times to keep my voice normal.*

"Okay...." Shane didn't look sure in the glow of the parking lot lights, but he walked to the other side of the car and got in.

Justin climbed in and started the car. He headed toward Shane's place. The silence inside the car was awkward, at best. This was not at all how he'd expected the night to end. Part of him was resigned while the other part was heartbroken.

The weekend before had been one of the best experiences of his life. Justin was falling hard for Shane, but tonight it had come to a screeching halt. The "good friend" introduction started it. Stuffing another man's phone number in his pocket finished it. Justin pulled into Shane's driveway and waited for him to get out.

"Are you feeling any better?" Shane asked from just outside the driver's door where he stopped. "You can stay at my place, if you want."

"Thanks, but I'm not good company tonight," Justin said without looking at him. "Shane.... Thank you for last weekend."

"Why does that sound like more than good night for the evening?" Shane sounded more confused than Justin had ever heard.

Seriously? Were they at the same bar? "I'll talk to you later. Good-bye, Shane." Justin backed out of Shane's driveway before he could argue. The time of holding himself together was past.

The sickness Justin feigned was very real now, complete with tight chest and nauseated stomach. He leaned toward the open window, trying to draw air into his lungs. Cool, autumn air stung his hot cheeks, but he welcomed the distraction on the ride home. The radio played so softly, Justin barely heard it. *Might as well enjoy it while I have it.* He reached down to raise the volume.

"Justin, this is the third message I've left today. You better be on your deathbed...." Shane was pissed, not to mention completely befuddled. When Justin left the night before, Shane had known something was wrong. He was kicking himself for not getting in his car and following Justin home.

Stomping from one end of the garage to the other, Shane growled at nothing and everything. He picked up a wrench and walked to the open hood of the Chevy he was doing a tune-up on. With one twist of his wrist, the wrench slipped and skin left his knuckles. "Fuck!"

"I see your language hasn't improved."

Shane jerked his head up and almost cracked it on the hood. He stepped to the left to see Lukas standing at the front of the building. "What are you doing here?"

"Hello to you too." Lukas chuckled.

"Sorry. I'm in a shit mood right now. You might consider running away." Shane half laughed.

"What's got your panties in a twist?" Lukas asked,

coming farther inside.

"Nothing," Shane said. "I think Justin's avoiding me again, and I don't know why."

"He said he was sick last night. Maybe he's sleeping." Lukas shrugged.

"Yeah, I guess...." Shane didn't think so, though. Something was wrong.

"You don't sound convinced...."

"It's private," Shane said.

Lukas put up his hands. "Sorry. Not my business. One more question and I'll change the subject."

"What?"

"Do you always get this fired up for a friend?" Lukas asked.

"He's more than a friend, Lukas."

"Oh, well, you didn't mention that last night," Lukas said. He moved in closer. "What are you doing to this one?"

"Tune-up, oil change. Routine maintenance," Shane said. "You're not working today?"

"I'm heading that way soon. I stopped by to see if you wanted to come in tonight so we could do more catching up." Lukas stuffed his hands in his pockets.

"We'll see. I should really go check on Justin."

"Whatever. I'm there all night." Lukas turned and started to leave. "If you were mine, I wouldn't ignore your calls...."

"What the fuck...?" Shane stared after him. *Did I wake up in some alternate universe, or has the world just gone crazy?*

SHANE WALKED INTO THE BAR AT A QUARTER AFTER

eight. The smile he greeted Lukas with was halfhearted, but it was the best he could muster. He'd tried calling Justin every hour on the hour all day long without any response. His texts went unanswered too. Shane had considered driving over to Justin's but thought better of it.

After Shane slid onto a stool and ordered a beer, Lukas brought him his drink and a plate of bacon ranch nachos. "Did you get the car done?"

"Yeah, the owner picked it up about an hour ago," Shane said, picking up a chip loaded with cheese and bacon. "This place is hopping tonight. Are you going to have time to visit?"

"Oh, sure. I'll make time." Lukas smiled.

"All right. So, tell me about how you ended up here," Shane said. Curiosity and the need for a distraction made him ask for the story. "Last I knew, you were supposed to be going to work for your father."

Lukas leaned his hip against the bar and nodded. "Did for a while. Hated it. I started moonlighting on weekends here, for excitement. Not that this place is the Hard Rock or anything. But it has a decent crowd on weekends, and it's somewhere my father would have never come looking for me. The old guy who ran this place turned it over to me to manage a few months after I started. When he finally was ready to sell it off, I had enough money in my trust to take it off his hands. It's been mine ever since." He laughed. "Dad about blew a gasket the day I gave him my notice."

"How are things with your dad now?" Shane asked.

"Room temperature, most days. He still doesn't get it or really approve, but he's resigned. I think he's hoping I fail and come crawling back so he can say he told me so. I'm determined to not let that happen," Lukas said.

"That sucks. Sorry he's acting that way," Shane said. He

remembered the man—tight assed, snobby, and the temper to match. Lukas had his sympathy on that front.

"It is what it is. Do you want a sandwich or something?" Lukas helped himself to a chip from Shane's plate.

"Sure. A burger with everything sounds good. And another beer." Shane drained the last third of his glass and set it toward Lukas. Loaded wasn't his goal, but a nice buzz would dull his frustration with Justin.

"*Yes, sir,*" Lukas said before walking away.

Lukas brought Shane a fresh beer. "Burger shouldn't take very long."

"No problem. I won't starve," Shane said, popping another chip into his mouth.

By the time the burger showed up, Shane had more than a buzz going. If he stared too long at something, it blurred, and he felt like the chair under him floated on water. He was sure he'd only had two beers, so why did he feel like he killed a case?

"Here, let me get you another beer," Lukas said.

"Thanks. Justin said you did carry out? Do you have a menu I can take with me? Your food is really good," Shane said. His voice sounded strange to his own ears, and his tongue felt thick. *Tongue. Justin. Mmmm.... He loved kissing Justin, especially with tongue. If Justin wanted to get his own way, Shane felt certain a few kisses would achieve that.*

"You can just call my cell, and I'll bring you whatever you want," Lukas said, placing another beer in front of Shane.

"That's really nice of you," Shane said. "You might regret that offer." He laughed.

Shane could have sworn he heard Lukas mumble "Doubt it."

15

BY THE time the bar closed, Shane was drunker than he could ever remember. He was aware of riding in a car, but he didn't recognize the neighborhood, at all. "Where are we?" Shane asked.

"We're home," Lukas said, pulling into the garage. "You shouldn't be alone right now."

"I'm fine...," Shane slurred.

"Yes, yes, you are." Lukas grinned at him.

"Are you flirting with me, Lukas?" Shane was confused. Something didn't feel right. Lukas was an old friend; Justin was his boyfriend, even if they hadn't talked all day.

"If you're not sure, I must not be doing it right." Lukas laughed and shook his head. He walked around the car and opened Shane's door. "Let's get you to bed."

"Bed, yeah. Sounds like a good idea." Shane stumbled out of the car and into Lukas's waiting arms. "My dick is hard...." He looked down and frowned.

"It's supposed to do that."

Lukas helped him into the house and into a bedroom he'd never seen before. When Lukas started undressing him, Shane tried to lift his hands to push him away, but arms didn't seem to work. Shane moaned in frustration. This was wrong.... But he was *so* horny. Justin—he wanted Justin.

Shane's clothes were finally off. He was hot and tired. At that point, Shane didn't care about whose bed it was, just that he wanted to stretch out and sleep. "Smile for Justin, Shane."

Shane did as Lukas said and then promptly fell asleep.

The next morning, Shane woke up with a monster headache. At first he blamed that for his disorientation. The more he blinked and focused, though, he realized he'd never seen this bedroom before.

Something brushed against his side, and he turned his head. Shane's stomach dropped when he saw Lukas sleeping beside him. *Oh no...* Shane tried not to move as he took inventory of his situation. The sheets against his body let him know he was naked—and in bed with someone he shouldn't have been. He closed his eyes and silently groaned. *What happened last night? Did I...? Justin will never forgive me for this, and I can't say as I would blame him.*

Shane was confused and felt dirty. Cheating was not something he would even consider if he was in his right mind, which made him wonder, again, what had happened the night before.

Shane was miserable, and he didn't even know

why. He knew the reason, just not the *why*. No matter how many times he checked his phone, the one call he wanted wouldn't come. Lukas called, though. Almost every day. When he didn't call, he dropped by. Sometimes Shane was grateful for the distraction, and other times he just wanted to be left alone.

Lukas didn't seem to be dissuaded by Shane's attitude. He didn't push, but Shane could read his intentions. Was Shane interested? He didn't know for certain. He was trying to make an effort, though. They'd slept together before Justin's scent had even left his sheets. Waking up in Lukas's bed had been a shock in the morning light. Guilt made Shane feel dirty, and that kept him from throwing himself into the relationship Lukas so obviously wanted.

THANKSGIVING AT THE WALKER HOUSE INVOLVED everyone pitching in, which was okay with Justin. He liked helping his mom in the kitchen. They'd had some of their best talks over the years while they worked.

"You seem down. Do you want to talk about it?" Justin's mom wore a look of concern mixed with curiosity.

He should have known she'd pick up on his mood. Justin looked down at the onion he was chopping. "Not really, but thanks." When his eyes welled with tears, he was grateful for the job he was doing. *Blame the onions.*

"Okay, but if you change your mind, I'm here. I won't judge," his mom said.

He huffed out a laugh and looked back up. "I think I've watched one too many conspiracy movies with you. I'm seeing ulterior motives where there aren't any."

"How so?" She looked even more curious now. Justin's mom had shared her love of mystery movies with him from a young age. The contests to see who could figure it out first were some of his most treasured memories.

"I had this friend. It seemed we both wanted more than friendship, but when an old flame came into the picture, he didn't choose me. Some things happened to make me back off and avoid them both, essentially pushing them together...."

The words poured out in a discombobulated mess until his mom held her hand up. "Start at the beginning and go slower, so I can keep up."

Justin sighed and sagged. "I had this friend. It turned out, we both wanted more than friendship."

She nodded. "Okay, I got that part. Go on."

"We went on a real date. We were going to eat dinner and dance the night away. But...." Justin paused to take a breath.

"But...?"

"The bartender was an old flame of Shane's. He wouldn't go away so we could be alone. Shane sort of forgot I was there. At least, that's how it felt," Justin said. "And he introduced me as his 'good friend.'"

"Oh, honey. I'm sorry. What happened next?"

"The longer it went on, the worse I felt. I just wanted to leave. So I pretended to be sick. Lukas brought the bill, I handed him my bank card. He came back and said it was declined. Mom, there was money in my account. I know there was." Justin pounded his fist on the counter, almost scattering the chopped onions.

"But this bartender said there wasn't?" His mom frowned.

"I know, right? Anyway, I avoided Shane the next day,

trying to get my head on straight. The truth was, Lukas was more Shane's type. Successful, gorgeous, they had a past," Justin said.

"Wait right there, young man. Are you telling me, you just walked away? Without fighting for your man?" He knew that look. She was about to get the switch.

"I—Mom...." He sighed. "I was falling hard. If I'd have let it go on longer, I would have had my heart broken worse than it is now."

"Justin Matthew Walker.... You're as good or better than this Lukas person." She growled. His mom actually growled at him. "What happened after that?"

"I got a nice little picture texted to me of Shane in a bed I didn't recognize, naked. The thing was, though, there was something strange about his expression—I can't put my finger on." Justin sighed again. While it kind of felt good to get this off his chest, it was also reopening the wound he was so desperately trying to close.

"You think they were deliberately trying to make you feel bad? Or they were telling you to back off? What did you do when you got the picture?" His mom was wringing and pulling the dish towel in her hand. She only did that when she was trying to figure something out.

"I did what any other person would do. I told Shane to never call me again and blocked his number and then ate a ton of ice cream." Justin turned to dump a pile of onions into the stuffing. Next he grabbed the celery and started pulling stalks off. "I don't like games, Mom. I especially don't like the ones where someone is trying to make someone else jealous— or whatever the intention with that picture was. If they wanted me gone from their lives, they got it."

His mother gave him a frown he'd seen many times in his

youth. It meant she didn't agree with his choice, but it was his life to screw up. Justin couldn't help it. He couldn't get the picture of Shane out of his head, even if there was something about it that bothered him.

16

"WHERE DID you go?" Lukas asked.

Shane was buried up to his eyeballs in paperwork. He'd been putting off doing it until he was caught up in the garage. "Huh?" He shook off his thoughts and focused on his visitor. "Oh, I was just thinking about my mom and what I should get her for Christmas."

"Oh, well, what are you thinking?"

"She loves the 49ers. I thought about getting her a jersey or something. Maybe a throw blanket. I wonder if she'd like to go to a game." Shane nodded. "I might look into their schedule later."

"Let me know if and when you get tickets, I'll give you money so you can get me a ticket too," Lukas volunteered.

"Oh, well, I was thinking it could be just the two of us, but if you want to come...."

"No, no... I understand. Go and have a good time," Lukas said, smiling.

Was Shane imagining it, or was the smile not quite reaching Lukas's eyes? Was Shane projecting his own misery onto the man in front of him? Sighing, he nodded and smiled. "Thanks for understanding."

"No problem. In all honesty, I'm envious of the relationship you have with your mother. I wish I had that kind of relationship with my father," Lukas said.

Using the mail opener, Shane opened the statement from Eddie's Auto Parts. "Still not going well?"

"Nothing's changed." Lukas shrugged.

Shane opened his mouth to say something, and what came out was *"What the fucking hell?"* He stood up, and his chair slammed back and into the wall behind him.

"What's wrong?" Lukas's eyes were wide.

Shane barely heard him over the pounding in his ears. "He returned it all! Everything! Hours we spent putting that radio in, and he just ripped it out?"

"He, who? What radio? Shane, what are you going on about?"

"I have to go. You'll let yourself out, right. I need to go see about this." Shane grabbed his flannel shirt from the back of the couch and left his office.

He left black marks decorating the street at the end of his driveway when he pulled out. Pissed didn't even come close. Those were gifts! It seemed Justin was cutting all ties with him, including anything to do with his car. Shane supposed he should be happy Justin hadn't used his school savings to pay for it instead. That would have put him right over the edge.

Parking in front of Eddie's, Shane shut off his car and went inside. "Is Eddie around?" he asked Hector.

"*Sí*, he's in the back. Want me to get him for you?" Hector said.

"No, I know the way. Thanks, though," Shane said. He

walked around the counter and down the aisle toward Eddie's office.

Calm. This isn't Eddie's fault.

"Shane! It's good to see you." Eddie stood up from his desk and moved to shake Shane's hand. "I wasn't expecting you today. Do you have a list for me?"

"It's good to see you too." Shane sat down in the chair across from Eddie and handed over the statement of his account. "No, I've come to ask about this. Are those negative returns?"

Eddie looked the statement over and nodded. "They are. A young man brought those back. You didn't send him?" He frowned.

"No, I didn't know anything about it. Did he say why he was returning the parts?" Shane asked.

"All he said was he didn't need them anymore since the car was sold," Eddie said.

Shane's stomach dropped to the floor. "He sold the car?"

Eddie shrugged. "I guess. That's what he said. What's wrong?"

Shane swallowed and shook his head. "Nothing. It's fine. My bill's smaller, right?" His laugh was weak to his own ears.

Eddie handed Shane's statement back and nodded with a smile. "A smaller bill is usually a good thing."

"Thanks, Eddie." Shane stood up and leaned over to shake Eddie's hand again. "I'll see you later."

17

"Bᴜᴛ I don't want to go out, Bobby," Justin huffed. He wanted to go home, shower, and fall into bed.

"Justin, man, you've been moping for weeks. It's time to go out and have some fun," his friend and coworker said.

"An hour, that's it." Justin gave in. Bobby was right. He had been moping for far too long. "Where we going?"

"You'll see. I'm driving." Bobby changed his shirt and moved toward the door. "C'mon. We'll eat, drink, and dance all our frustrations out."

Justin felt a pang of guilt. He'd been so absorbed in his own misery, had he missed something with Bobby? "Our? What are you frustrated about?"

Bobby shrugged and laughed. "The usual. No hot body warming my bed. Hand cramps."

Justin barked out a laugh. Bobby was a vulgar shit. But he was a funny, harmless vulgar shit. "You should learn to use the other hand."

Bobby snorted. "And look like Popeye. No thanks."

They were still laughing when they got into Bobby's car.

It wasn't much nicer than Justin's used POS, but it did lack the puke-green exterior. A pang of regret hit Justin in the chest. He missed his Mustang, but selling it had been a means to an end. The extra money he had now would make it less stressful to cut his work hours and start school sooner.

When Bobby pulled up outside Lukas's bar, Justin's stomach rolled. "I don't think I can go in here, Bobby." What if Lukas and Shane were there? Would he be able to handle watching them together? If he were honest with himself, the answer was a solid no.

"Why not?" Bobby wanted to know.

Justin gave him the highlights of the Shane saga and then folded his hands in his lap. They were shaking. His heart was pounding. Justin thought about that picture again. What he wouldn't give to have that wiped from his mind. He had finally realized the strange look on Shane's face in that picture was Shane drunk. It didn't make the hurt and betrayal less, though. He'd been avoiding all places where he might run into Shane or Lukas, and where did Bobby bring him? To the one place the most likely to see one or both.

"Oh, sorry. I knew something was up with you, but I didn't know it was like that," Bobby said sympathetically. "So, you're going to let them win and hide like a scared child? I have to tell you, Justin, I thought you were tougher than that."

"Nice try, Bobby. Challenging my manhood isn't going to make me go in there with a swagger. Why don't you say something about the size of my dick? Don't think that will work either, but you could give it a shot."

"Okay. Your dick is so small...."

"Enough," Justin said, laughing. "Fine, but if it gets bad, we leave, okay?"

"Sure thing," Bobby said.

He had a bad feeling about this—a really bad feeling. Sighing, he climbed from the car and followed Bobby to the door. The music pumped through the bar's speakers so loud the floor vibrated under their feet. Dodging bodies around the pool table and bumping into others dancing, they found their way to an empty table in the back. They slid onto chairs, Justin with his back to the wall. He scanned the crowd for familiar faces, but the only one he recognized was the waitress who sometimes delivered to him during the week. She caught his eye and gave him a smile and nod before starting through the bar toward them.

"Hey, handsome. Are you eating or drinking, or both?"

"Both," Bobby said.

Tiffany glanced at Bobby, then turned her focus back to Justin. "Ready or do you need a minute?"

"I'm ready. Bring me a beer and a plate of onion rings with horseradish dip, please," Justin said, smiling.

"Give me something fruity with an umbrella and an order of nachos," Bobby said.

"I'll put your food order in and bring your drinks right back." Tiffany bounced away.

"It's too bad we don't go for chicks. She seemed interested in you," Bobby said.

"Maybe I should switch teams," Justin said with a laugh.

18

SHANE TAPPED on the steering wheel absently with the beat of his heart. The radio's music had faded from his notice long ago.

Where the hell is he?

Shane's last stop had been Justin's job, but he had no idea what Justin's new car looked like. So he'd gone inside to take a leak while scoping out the employees. No Justin, that he could see. Now he was at Justin's place, sitting outside in his car like a stalker. No lights were on in Justin's apartment, and his car's parking space was empty. Shane had been there almost an hour, with no signs of life. A chirp behind him and red and blue lights in his rearview mirror woke him from his stupor.

Fuck me running....

A flashlight beam bounced closer to the driver's door. "License, please."

"Yes, sir. Is there a problem, officer?" Shane fished his wallet out of his pocket and handed over his license to the policeman.

"Tenants across the street called and said a suspicious man was sitting outside in his car for an hour. They were a bit concerned you were casing the joint. Are you?" The officer handed Shane's license back.

"Am I what?" Shane asked, frowning.

"Casing the joint," the officer said, smirking.

"No, sir. I'm just waiting for my b—er—friend to get home. He's late," Shane said.

"I suggest you move along and give him a call later." The officer stepped back from Shane's door. "If I come back around the block and you're still here, I'm ticketing you for illegal parking and loitering."

Shane sighed and straightened in his seat. "Yes, sir...."

"You have a good night." The policeman walked back to his cruiser and climbed in. The bright red and blue lights turned off, but his car didn't move.

"Fine, fine." Shane mumbled, starting his car. He pulled out from his parking place and started down the street. The police car followed him to the next intersection and then turned off.

Jail or a ticket didn't seem like it would be the highlight of his day. *I'll go back to his job and see if I missed him. At least, maybe I can find out which car is Justin's.*

The trip to Justin's work put Shane in an even more foul mood. No one there would give him any information about Justin or his whereabouts. Only that he'd left with some guy named Bobby. If Shane wasn't careful, he'd be seeing the inside of a jail cell, after all.

"WHAT ARE YOU DOING HERE?"

Justin looked up in surprise. "I didn't know I was banned."

Lukas laughed, but it didn't reach his eyes. He mock hit Justin on the bicep. "Of course you're not banned. Is Tiffany taking good care of you and your friend?"

Justin smiled. "She is."

"Good, good. Let me know if there's anything you need," Lukas said before leaving them alone.

Justin and Bobby laughed, danced, and ate. Justin hadn't expected to have a good time, but he really was enjoying himself. While the speakers thumped and they danced, he could forget all the negatives in his life.

When the music slowed to a ballad, Bobby headed back to the table. Justin turned in the opposite direction for the restroom. A quick piss, and then he washed his hands. He was turning off the water in the sink when he heard a voice behind him.

"Waiting for me? I guess you'll do...."

Justin whipped around with wide eyes. "What?"

"You think this will be the first time I've hooked up in this bathroom?" Lukas moved toward Justin, reaching for his waist.

Justin backed up. "What are you doing?"

"Don't play hard to get. We're both too old for those games. I just want a little taste of what you gave Shane. He doesn't even have to know." Lukas reached out again. This time he grabbed Justin's dick.

Justin slapped Lukas's hand away and shifted his hips. "Get away from me, Lukas."

Lukas laughed. "Guys like you and I know the score, Justin. We fuck; we walk away." He crowded Justin against the wall and bracketed him with a hand on either side of his head. "Now, let's get this party started before someone walks in."

Justin raised his hands and pushed against Lukas's chest. "I said, get away from me. I mean it."

He wasn't expecting the slap across his face, though maybe he should have. It wouldn't be the first time someone had used him for a punching bag. Stars danced in front of his eyes for a second before Justin blinked to clear them. Struggling to get away, he lifted his leg, but either his aim was off or Lukas had expected it, because Justin barely caught him in the thigh.

Lukas balled up his fist and punched Justin in the stomach. Justin's breath shot out in a whoosh as he doubled over.

"I don't know what Shane saw in you other than you're kind of pretty."

"You're an asshole, Lukas." Justin wheezed.

"I didn't tell you to speak. Although, your mouth would serve the purpose, and I know it's not the first time you've got on your knees in a bar bathroom." Lukas sneered. "Get down and open your pretty little mouth for me."

"Screw you."

"See, I'm much more Shane's type, while you're nothing more than a piece of ass."

"Justin, you fall in, man...." Bobby walked into the restroom and froze. He looked between the two of them and frowned. "What's going on here?"

"No-Nothing. Let's go, Bobby," Justin stuttered.

"Yes, Bobby. Take your girlfriend here and go. He's no longer welcome in my bar," Lukas said.

Bobby stared at Lukas hard for a second. "All right...."

Lukas shrugged. "He came at me first. I was defending myself."

"Yeah. Right," Bobby said, opening the door for Justin.

19

"ARE YOU okay? What the hell was that all about?" Bobby's voice rose with every word. "Do you need to go to the hospital?"

"Yes. It's complicated. I don't think so." Justin wanted to go home; he wanted to go see Shane. He wanted to think, but Bobby's freaking out wasn't making that possible.

"This isn't funny, Justin. If I hadn't walked in when I did, it could have been a lot worse," Bobby said.

That was true. "Thank you for that, by the way."

"I'm not looking for thanks. What's going on?" Bobby pulled into the parking space beside Justin's car.

"That was Shane's new boyfriend. I apparently looked good enough for a quickie in the bathroom," Justin said flatly.

"*What?* I'm so confused," Bobby said. He frowned at Justin. "If he's Shane's boyfriend, why was he putting moves on you?"

"You're not the only one. Was it me, or did Lukas's eyes seem weird?" He couldn't get the furious, crazy look out of his head. Justin would have been afraid of Lukas if he hadn't been so angry.

"Now that you mention it, yeah." Bobby's voice had returned to a reasonable volume.

"I think he meant to rape me." Justin ground his back teeth together until it hurt.

"Whoa. Are you going to tell Shane? It could break them up," Bobby said.

"That's what I'm afraid of. What if Shane didn't believe me and thought I was only trying to break them up?" Justin sagged in his seat. All of a sudden, he was exhausted. "I don't know what to do, Bobby. I'm not going to tell Shane to get him back, but I am worried about his safety."

"Because you don't know what Lukas is capable of." Bobby nodded. "You have to tell Shane."

"I know," Justin said. He sighed and opened the car door. "I can't deal with anything more tonight. Tomorrow, I'll go see Shane—or call him."

"You sure you're okay to drive?" Bobby asked.

"Yeah, I'm good. I'm going straight home and crawl into bed," Justin said, climbing out.

"I'll follow you home, just to be sure." Bobby's voice was firm. Many people thought Bobby was flighty because of the way he acted, but Justin knew better.

"If you insist...." Justin closed the car door and climbed into his own ride. He hadn't bothered to lock his car, hoping someone would steal the ugly thing, but no such luck so far. After starting the engine, he pulled out of his spot and headed for home. Ibuprofen and his bed were calling his name....

· · ·

IT WAS AFTER MIDNIGHT. WHERE THE HELL WAS JUSTIN?

For fuck's sake, I sound like the man's mom. I guess this Bobby person is good company.

Every time Shane remembered Justin was out with *Bobby*, his temper flared hot. Jealous? Hell yeah, he was. In the back of his mind, a reasonable voice said he had no right to be. Shane squashed that voice. Right or not, it was how he felt.

After the cop incident earlier, Shane gave up the parking and waiting gig. Instead he drove past Justin's place every fifteen minutes, taking different routes so the neighbors wouldn't call the police again. Until the clock hit eleven thirty. By then, hopefully the worrying neighbors were in bed and it was safe to park. To be sure, though, he parked at the end of the block where he had a clear view of Justin's place, should any lights come on.

A half hour of talking to himself and envisioning Justin with someone else had him shifting restlessly in his seat. Shane wanted to get out and pace, but that didn't seem the best idea. Another half hour, and he said, "Fuck it."

Shane got out of his car, locked the doors, and marched up to Justin's front door. No one was home yet, so he didn't knock, but he did park his ass on the front stoop to wait. He didn't sit there long before the ugliest car he'd ever seen in his life pulled into Justin's parking space.

You've got to be kidding me....

Shane watched Justin climb from his car and start toward him. He knew the moment Justin spotted him sitting there. Justin halted midstep, and then sighed before continuing toward him. Shane stood up to meet him.

"We need to talk." He didn't mean for it to come out as a demand. *Yes, I did.*

Justin tensed and shook his head. "No. We don't." He stepped past Shane to unlock his door. "Go away. I'm too tired for this."

Shane's hackles rose, immediately thinking Justin was too tired because of something illicit. "You can skip the details on my account, thanks." He followed Justin into the apartment without an invitation.

"Get out of my house, Shane." Justin's tone never wavered, rose, or showed any kind of emotion.

"Not until we talk. I wanna know what's going on, Justin." Now that Justin was home safely and—Shane wasn't ashamed to admit this—alone, some of Shane's adrenaline had fallen off.

"What's going on with what?"

"Whose piece of shit are you driving? Where's your car?"

Justin flipped on the kitchen light and disappeared from Shane's view. "That is my car."

"I'm sorry. Did you say that fugly car is yours?" Shane walked into the kitchen after Justin.

"Yup. Bought and paid for," Justin said before taking a long drink from a soda bottle. Shane frowned. It wasn't Justin's usual brand of soda, instead one of the store off-brands. Was Justin hurting for money? Did something happen with his parents? Now he was more concerned than angry.

"What's going on?" Shane asked, softer this time.

Justin turned to face him, and Shane saw the bruise forming on Justin's jaw. "What the fuck happened to you? Did you get in a fight?"

"Well, since you answered your own question, I guess I don't need to be here for this conversation." Justin started to stomp past Shane.

Shane grabbed his arm to halt him. "Who and why? Did this new guy do this to you? I'll break him in half."

"What new guy? Why do you care? Go home, Shane. It's late and I'm tired." Justin tried to pull free and then hissed.

Shane dropped Justin's arm like it was on fire. "What? Where are you hurt? I didn't have hold of you that tight."

"I'm fine," Justin said, walking away.

"What did I tell you about lying to me?" Shane ground out.

"That was when I thought we had a chance at something. Now, I don't have to listen to you. You're not my dad," Justin shouted.

"Stop acting like a child." Shane was shocked. Justin had never raised his voice at him before. He'd never seen Justin angry before. If Shane wasn't concerned and angry himself, he might have thought it kind of hot. "Dad or not, I want an explanation. Why did someone hit you?"

"Because of you, Shane!" Justin's face fell before he mouthed the word "Fuck."

Shane's eyebrows rose. "Because of me? What do you mean?"

"Nothing. Never mind. Why aren't you gone yet?" Justin said flatly.

"Oh, no. I'm not leaving until you tell me everything. The car, the fight, the soda, all of it." Shane folded his arms across his chest.

"Soda? What?"

20

Justin was starting to wonder if Shane was drunk. He was making no sense. Why was he even there? Justin told him to leave at least three times. Did the man not understand English?

"The soda is the last thing I want explained," Shane said. "You can start with the fight and how it was my fault."

"I don't want to talk about it right now. I'm too tired to deal with you," Justin said before spinning on his heel and marching from the living room. *Maybe he'll take the hint and leave.*

"Deal with me? When did talking to me change from a pleasant experience to dealing with me?" Shane asked from behind him. He was too close to not have followed him.

Piss and vinegar! "Several weeks ago." Justin sat down on the bed and bent to take off his shoes. He grunted and bounced back up to sitting when he touched the sore ribs.

"Here," Shane said, coming to kneel in front of Justin.

"Thanks," Justin said. He watched Shane unlace and

pull off one shoe and then the other. "What are you doing here, Shane?" His voice was quiet. There wasn't any demand in it. Justin didn't want to fight anymore. He didn't even want to talk. What he wanted, he couldn't have.

"You haven't talked to me for weeks. I got the statement today with the credits on it. You sold your car. You loved that car.... Noisy doors and all." Shane looked up at him with questions in his eyes.

"I'm going to school. By selling my car and watching my spending, I had enough saved to start a semester earlier than I planned," Justin said. "I should have warned you, but I wasn't even sure you'd talk to me." He shrugged and looked away.

"Don't do that. I hate it when you do that, like you're ashamed or something." Shane was frowning when Justin turned his head back.

"Kicked Puppy Syndrome."

"What?" Shane asked.

"Kicked Puppy Syndrome. At a certain point, puppies who are kicked a lot learn to expect to get kicked. So, they flinch and back up before it can happen." Justin gave a sad smile. "I'm sure it has some other fancy, clinical name but mine fits."

"I see." Shane sat back on his haunches for a moment, just staring at Justin.

"What?" Justin frowned at him.

"Nothing. I was just letting it sink in." Shane pushed up off the floor and held out a hand. "Stand up and let me help you undress."

Oh, hell no! No way he was going to let Shane undress him. A woody was absolutely not appropriate at the moment. "Um, no thanks. I can manage."

"Are you sure? I don't mind helping you," Shane said. His hand was still outstretched.

Justin couldn't resist touching, so he took Shane's hand and let Shane help him to his feet. The grunting was kept to a minimum, thank goodness. They stood there, awkwardly staring at each other with their hands joined. Neither moved, nor looked away. Justin could feel his heart hammering. He needed to pull away. He should really move away, like, to the other side of the room. But he couldn't force himself to do anything but look into the eyes of the man he wasn't close to being over. "Shane...."

Shane closed the distance between them. Justin could feel Shane's breath on his face. He could smell the hint of coffee and peppermint gum on his breath. Justin was sure this was a mistake, but he couldn't make himself care. "Please...."

Justin didn't stop him when Shane lowered his head to touch his lips to Justin's. Though he should have, instead of practically begging for it. It was barely a brush before Shane straightened. "I'm going before I can't pull away. I will be back tomorrow morning, and you will be answering my questions, Justin."

"If I'd known kissing me would get you to leave, I'd have kissed you on the sidewalk," Justin said.

"Nice," Shane said with a shake of his head. He turned to leave. "Tomorrow, and don't think of avoiding me."

"There he is." Tiffany grinned as Shane walked up to the bar.

"What's up?" Shane said.

"What's up? The sky. Clouds. The temperature and

hormone levels in here." She laughed. "Where have you been? I figured we'd see you before now."

"I had something I needed to do, first," Shane answered. "Is Lukas here?"

"Yeah, he's back in his office," Tiffany said. "You want me to get him?"

"Nah, I'll go on back." Shane smiled at her. "Thanks, though."

"Don't do anything I wouldn't do."

Shane walked around the bar and back through the kitchen. He wasn't looking forward to the conversation, but it wasn't fair to Lukas—leading him on. He had tried, but his heart wasn't in it. Something that was made abundantly clear tonight.

Lukas's office door was closed. Shane knocked and walked on in. He froze in place when he saw what Lukas was doing. The man was half hunched over his desk, a line of white powder in front of him and a straw in his hand. *"What the hell?"*

"Well, well. If it isn't high-and-mighty Shane, rearing his ugly head." Lukas laughed. "Justin run to tattle on me? I figured he'd spill the beans, probably making it out worse than it was."

"Tattle? Spill the beans?" *What was Lukas talking about?* "Not exactly," Shane said. "Why don't you tell me your side?"

"I was only playing. I didn't know he'd get so worked up about a little touchy-feely in the restroom." Lukas shrugged.

"What?" Shane deadpanned.

"Well, it wasn't like you were putting out, even after the roofie. How was I supposed to know you'd get as out of it as you did? Shit, man. I didn't even get laid—twice now—and do you know how much that one little pill cost me?" Lukas sighed and then laughed. "You should have seen the look on that little bastard's face when I grabbed his package. I thought the pussy was going to cry."

Shane tried to keep the shock and anger from his expression when he nodded. Lukas was telling him everything he wanted to know, and more. "I see."

"I knew you'd understand. He's not good enough for you," Lukas said.

"What's up with the stuff in front of you?" Shane patted himself on the back for keeping his tone even.

Lukas raised his injured hand. "Painkillers weren't strong enough."

"What happened to your hand?" Tonight was one revelation after another. Lukas looked way too sure of himself for this to be the first time he'd snorted.

"I hit a wall. My temper got the best of me after you ran out to check on Justin," Lukas said.

"Ah. Yeah. I'm sorry about that." He had been, but not so much now.

"It'll heal. Are you going to come over here and kiss it better?" Lukas's expression turned flirtatious.

"Mmmm... I don't think so. I think my kissing any part of you is at an end. Stay away from me, and stay away from Justin." Shane turned to leave.

"Wait. What?"

"You crossed so many lines tonight, I don't even know where to begin, Lukas. You should count yourself lucky I haven't knocked you into next week." Shane opened the door. "Good-bye."

Shane closed the door against Lukas's sputtering protests. How the hell did he fix the problems Lukas had helped him make? He'd go home and sleep on it before going back to Justin's.

PAIN RICOCHETED through the side of his face. For the few hours he slept, Justin forgot the disaster from the night before. More pain, this time in his ribs, brought a grunt as he sat up in his bed. Would it be too much to hope that Shane didn't show up? Probably.

After a hot shower and a little caffeine, Justin started to feel a bit more human. His jaw had a slight discoloration, but going with the scruffy look for a few days should hide it from his coworkers and the public. Bobby texted to see how he was and seemed satisfied with the "I'm fine" response Justin sent.

Justin was flipping through the channels on the television when a knock came at his door. Ten o'clock. *I'm surprised he waited this long.*

Pushing up off the couch, he shuffled to the front door. It took everything he had not to run. Toward the door or away from it was a question he chose to ignore. "What? Didya oversleep?"

"Be nice or I won't feed you," Shane said, walking in past

Justin. There was a different air about him from the night before.

Justin pushed the door shut and sighed. "I'm always nice." He followed Shane into the kitchen. "What did you bring?"

"Contraband." Shane handed him a large bottle of his favorite soda.

Justin didn't know what to say. "You think I can be bribed?"

"No, I'm hungry, and I didn't want to give you time to hide. So we eat. Then we talk," Shane said.

"There you go, being bossy again." Justin took his soda and went to sit at the small kitchen table.

Shane sat down across from him and started handing out food. "For future reference, can you?"

"Can I what?" Justin frowned at him.

"Be bribed." Shane bit into his sandwich and met Justin's gaze.

Justin shrugged. "Possibly. It has to be better than a soda, though. I'm not cheap."

Shane choked on his sandwich and then laughed. "Good to know."

Butterflies did the mambo in Justin's stomach. He'd been fighting to get past the feelings for Shane, thinking they'd only see each other by chance. But here Shane was, bringing him breakfast and teasing him from across the table. What was this? What about Lukas?

Speaking of.... Justin needed to come clean about the night before. What would that do to the current easiness?

"What's with the look?"

He broke from his inner turmoil at the sound of Shane's voice. "What look?"

"Never mind. So tell me about school," Shane said before taking a drink of his coffee.

Justin perked up. "I start in a couple of weeks. I rearranged my work schedule to fit around it."

"Are you cutting back on hours?"

"Not much. Just working more early morning shifts and all weekend."

"When will you study?"

"When I'm not at work or in class," Justin said.

"Okay, and when will you sleep?" Shane asked. He was looking hard now.

"My first semester classes aren't that hard. I won't need as much study time as you're thinking." Justin stood up and started clearing their mess.

"I'm not accusing," Shane said before helping. "Just wondering how you're going to manage it all."

"People do it all the time. I'll be fine." Justin shrugged. He was determined, focused, and going after something he wanted with a passion. He could sleep between semesters.

"I know."

So many mistakes. So much time lost. Shane thought if they hadn't been manipulated by Lukas, it would be the perfect time for Justin to move in. Getting back to where they were wouldn't be easy. It might not happen at all. But Shane had hope... and a stranglehold on his need to demand something he had no right to demand.

"You know?" Justin frowned at him.

"This isn't a whim for you. You'll make it work. Just know, I'm here if you need anything." Shane meant it too. He didn't care if Justin needed help with homework or an emergency ride at three in the morning.

"Thank you." The frown faded from Justin's face.

"You're welcome." Shane smiled. "You wanna move this party to the couch?"

"Sure. Follow me," Justin said, turning on his heel.

I'd follow you anywhere.

They sat at opposite ends on the couch. Justin avoided looking at him. Shane hated when he did that. "I think we've put this off long enough. Justin, last night...." Shane sighed. Part of him wanted to hear Justin tell the story. But all of him wanted to apologize for every day of their time apart.

"There are some things I need to tell you, but I don't want you to think they're me trying to get you back," Justin said. "I'm not."

That stung. "Justin...."

"No, I need to tell you." The misery was clear in Justin's eyes when he looked over. "Lukas and I had an... incident last night. He, uh, made a pass at me. I told him no, and he tried to force the issue. I'm not sure, but he seemed... out of it."

"I know," Shane said.

Justin didn't react or stop talking. He rambled about everything, confirming Lukas's story. The more Justin said, the further Shane's stomach fell and the harder his heart pounded. "Justin. I know. You don't have to say any more."

"You know? How?" Justin's brows drew down.

"Lukas told me when I found him doing a line last night," Shane said.

"'Doing a line'? Coke?"

Shane nodded. "Yup. I didn't have any idea he was like that."

"Well, I'm sure with your support he can kick the habit." Justin nodded.

"That'll be hard, since I told him to stay away from you and me both."

Justin's eyebrows shot up. "You did? But I thought...."

Shane shrugged. "Trust is a deal breaker for me. Drugs too."

The breath rushed from Justin. "Okay. Good."

"Okay, good?" Shane barked a laugh. "Which part is 'okay' and which is the 'good' part?" Shane watched Justin's cheeks turn red. He chuckled, again.

"That didn't come out right. What I meant was, I'm glad I won't have to worry anymore," Justin said.

"You can worry a little, if you want. I could drop a car on my foot, or conk myself in the head with a wrench," Shane teased.

"I thought you knew what you were doing? Shouldn't you know how not to do those things?" Justin laughed.

"Ha. Ha. Accidents do happen. That's why they're called 'accidents.'"

22

"I'M SORRY about last night, Justin. I feel like this is all my fault, like you said." Shane sighed.

Justin frowned. "I was hurt, angry, and maybe a little anxious. I didn't mean it."

"But you were right. I wonder what else Lukas did that I don't know about." Shane paced the length of the living room.

"You know about the picture, right?" Justin asked, watching him.

"Picture? What picture?" Shane stopped pacing to frown at Justin.

"The one from the night you spent at his place."

"Still don't know what you're talking about."

"I was sent a naked picture of you in Lukas's bed. You looked drunk." Justin looked away. The memory still hurt.

"Apparently I was drugged with a roofie. Explains why I don't remember much of that night," Shane said. "We didn't have sex, Justin, just so you know."

"You just said you don't remember much of that night. How do you know?" Justin asked.

"Lukas told me when he was blabbing everything last night." Shane smiled.

"Do you believe him?" Justin nodded as some of the pain and anger started to fade. Lord knew, he wanted to believe they hadn't slept together.

"I can't be 100 percent sure, but, Justin... I wouldn't have knowingly cheated on you. I don't play that way."

After a moment's hesitation, Justin realized, regardless of Lukas's lies, he believed in Shane. "Do you want to stay and watch a movie, or do you have something else you need to do?" He tried to keep his face neutral, while his heart raced. *Please say yes.*

"No, I'm actually caught up with work at the garage, and I'm procrastinating on finishing my paperwork." Shane stretched his legs out in front of him and leaned farther back into the couch. "What movie?"

"Let's see what's on demand." Leaning forward, he grabbed the remote and turned on the television.

"Nothing sad. I'd hate for you to see me ugly cry." Shane batted his lashes.

Justin couldn't contain the laughter. Sweet and innocent was definitely not Shane. "I think I'd enjoy seeing that. Let me see if I can find *The Notebook.*"

"No! Not that! Anything but that!" Shane burst out laughing.

"Oh, look! A *Fast and Furious* marathon." Justin grinned at Shane. "Vin Diesel is so hot."

Shane narrowed his eyes and growled. "You think so, huh?"

Justin considered Shane for a moment before he answered. "You remind me of him, a little."

"How?" Shane asked.

"Big, bald, and badass."

A slow smile spread across Shane's face. He began to chuckle. "I can live with that."

Justin grinned. "Of course you can."

Halfway through the second movie, they dozed off. Awareness tried to pull Justin from his thoroughly enjoyable nap. He burrowed further into the delicious-smelling pillow, and then hummed his pleasure.

The pillow his face was pressed into wiggled. He frowned until his brain kicked in. His pillow wasn't wiggling; Shane was laughing. Justin groaned and sat up. "Sorry...," he mumbled.

"Sorry for what? Drooling on my shirt?"

Justin jerked his head up to see the damage while Shane laughed harder. "I'm kidding! You didn't drool on me, and I wouldn't have cared if you did. Goof."

"Asshole." Justin smirked.

SHANE HAD BEEN SURPRISED TO FIND JUSTIN LYING across his chest when he woke up. He had to fight against playing his fingers through Justin's curls. Justin's hair was a little longer than he usually kept it, but Shane liked the change. Somehow, it made the green of his eyes pop more.

When Justin buried his face in Shane's chest, something between a laugh and groan threatened. The soft noise he made had Shane trying to swallow the amusement. He managed to stay silent, but he couldn't hold his chest still.

The trust Justin felt in his sleep gave Shane hope for

their future. He knew they were attracted; he knew they could get along. What he didn't know was whether Justin would be willing to try again.

SHANE PULLED UP IN FRONT OF JUSTIN'S. AFTER THEIR nap, they'd decided they were hungry. Justin had offered to cook, but a quick look in the fridge revealed nothing promising. So Shane ordered Chinese and went to pick it up.

He expected Justin to come out to help or at least to be waiting at the door for him. Juggling bags, Shane grabbed the door handle, but the apartment was locked. *Weird.* He pounded on the door, but there was no response. Justin's car was in its space, so he hadn't left.

Something felt off. Shane couldn't hear anything from inside when he called for Justin. When the police car pulled up, Shane let out a string of curses.

"You again. What do you have against these neighbors?" the officer asked.

"Nothing, why?"

"Someone called and said you were out here making a racket." The policeman looked ready to pull out his cuffs.

"I don't know who told you what, but I'm glad you're here. Something is wrong." Shane set the bags on the stoop beside the door. "No one is answering the door."

"Maybe your friend left? Or maybe you aren't wanted here."

"No. I went to get dinner. Justin knew I was coming back, and his car is still here." Shane pointed to the ugly green car.

"Let me try." The officer was dubious, but at least he

wasn't completely blowing Shane off. He pounded on the door and identified himself.

No answer.

The neighbor's door opened and a scowling older woman stepped out. "This is ridiculous. What does a woman have to do to get peace around here?"

"Ma'am, we're sorry for disturbing you, but have you seen anyone go in and out of this place?"

"I saw this one leave and then another man go in. I'm going to have to complain to the manager," she said. "This isn't some gay brothel. We're a respectable neighborhood."

"Another man? Who?" Shane demanded.

The cop tossed a glare at Shane, and he glared back. This was his life they were talking about, damn it.

"Well, I don't know his name. I didn't ask," she said, disdain obvious.

"But you didn't see either of them come out?" the policeman asked.

"No. What do you think I do, stand in the window all day?" she scowled at both of them. "I wouldn't have noticed, if they hadn't been having some lovers' quarrel." She muttered, "Disgraceful."

"So they were fighting?" the officer asked.

"Now do you believe me? Do something. Break the door down, or I will." Shane started to turn.

"Don't make me put you in cuffs, Mr. Steel."

Shane balled his fists before giving the officer a curt nod. *For fuck's sake.* He looked at the old woman. "What did he look like?"

She sniffed and glanced at the cop, then looked Shane up and down before responding. "I don't know. Like some street hood but built like you. I wasn't paying that much attention."

Yeah, right. Shane didn't buy that for a minute. By the look on the cop's face, he didn't either. He turned to Shane. "Do you know anyone like that?"

"I don't know. Yeah, probably." Shane thought about it for a moment. Lukas was the first person to come to mind, but surely not....

"Ma'am, did you notice his hair color? Was he black, white, Hispanic?"

"Oh, he was definitely white."

Getting answers out of her was like pulling teeth. Shane fought not to walk over and shake her. "Can we stop screwing around here and go see about Justin now? Damn."

"Watch your mouth, young man. I'm a lady." She propped her hands on her hips.

"Lady, if you don't start talking, far worse words are going to come out of my mouth," Shane said.

The old busybody's jaw dropped. Apparently she wasn't used to people talking back. "Well, I never!" She looked at the policeman. "Are you just going to stand there? He can't talk to me that way."

"Let's everyone calm down...."

"Calm down? My boyfriend might be getting murdered in there, and we're all standing around with our thumbs in our asses!" Shane turned away and started for the door again.

"Smoke! I smell smoke," Shane said before ramming his shoulder against the door.

The cop looked like he didn't believe him, but after a second, he joined Shane in trying to break in the door. It took three hits before the lock broke.

Shane ran inside with the officer on his heels. They checked room by room, calling for Justin until they came to the bedroom. Shane stared in shock.

"Why couldn't you just walk away?" Lukas stood behind Justin, one arm wrapped around his neck and a gun in his other hand.

"Because I love him," Shane said. He clenched and unclenched his fists while his heart raced. No, it wouldn't end this way. Shane had to do something.

The officer had his own weapon drawn, pointed at Lukas and Justin. "Put the gun down. You haven't hurt anyone yet."

Lukas glanced at him. "No. If he's out of my way, I can have Shane back."

"No, wait. Let Justin go and you can have me now."

"You're lying. You just said you loved him!" Lukas's voice rose.

"But he doesn't love me, Lukas. Right, Justin?" Shane hoped Justin read the pleading in his eyes.

"No. No, I don't. I don't want anything to do with Shane," Justin croaked.

"You looked awfully cozy on the couch for not wanting anything to do with each other," Lukas said.

He'd seen them? How long had he been watching them? Lukas had the same glassy look as the night in his office. He was high or drunk or both. Could they reason with someone out of his head?

"Lukas. That's your name?" the officer said.

"Yeah. You need to go. This is between us," Lukas said.

"I'm sorry. I can't do that, Lukas."

"Go! Now!" He tightened his arm around Justin's throat until Justin's face started turning red.

"Okay, okay. I'm backing off." The cop stepped back and out of Lukas's sight. He walked away until he could radio for backup without being heard.

Shane stayed in the doorway. "Lukas, please. Let Justin go. He can't breathe."

"Good. Not breathing means he won't be in my way." Lukas pushed the muzzle of the gun against Justin's temple.

JUSTIN CHOKED ON A WHIMPER. WITH THE ARM AROUND his neck, he was barely getting air. It wouldn't be long until he passed out at this rate. *Have to be strong.* When Lukas had pushed his way into his home, Justin had expected a beating. With the gun pressed against his head, he wished for that beating now. He'd seen this situation countless times in movies. Justin figured he had a fifty-fifty chance of walking away.

He thought of his mom and dad. If he died today, they'd be devastated. And what about Shane? The guilt would eat him alive. Whether they'd have made a relationship work or not, Shane was doing his best to talk Lukas down. He would feel he failed if Justin didn't survive.

"LUKAS! HE'S NOT IN YOUR WAY! I WALKED AWAY because of the drugs. You know, goody-goody that I am." Shane shrugged, pretending calm when he felt anything but. "Quit the drugs and I'm all yours."

Lukas looked unsure. "Really? You mean that?" He started scowling again. "I still think we'd be better off without this one."

"If you kill him, you'll be in jail forever. We'll never have a chance to be together," Shane reasoned. He wondered if logic would even register with Lukas. Shane hoped so.

"You have a point...."

Shane swallowed his anger and fear. The situation was already too tense without his emotions to make it worse. "I mean it. Let Justin go and let's be together."

Lukas seemed to be mulling that over. The front door opened behind Shane, making Lukas focus again. "How 'bout I just kill him and make sure of it?"

With a quick look, Shane could see two more officers in SWAT gear enter the apartment. If he didn't talk Lukas down, this could end badly for everyone.

"Lukas." Shane took a step farther into the room. "Baby. There's one too many people in this room. What I have to say to you should be just between us."

"You think I'm stupid? I know you are just trying to save your little boy toy."

"I'm not. He's served his purpose, and I'm done. I need someone stronger... like you." Shane forced confidence into his voice.

Lukas's glazed eyes focused on Shane's face. A small smile started on his lips. "Yeah? Okay." He loosened his grip on Justin and pushed him away. His focus was all for Shane, just as Shane wanted it.

"Go Justin. Get out of here. This is about Lukas and me now." Shane saw Justin hesitate for a second before scrambling past him and out the door. "Okay, Lukas, it's just us so you can put the gun down, right?"

"Oh. Right." Lukas dropped the gun to the bed and stepped toward Shane.

Shane punched him square in the nose, knocking him on his ass. "You bastard. I hope you rot in jail, if I don't kill you first." He dove on top of Lukas and gripped his head to bang it against the floor. "Never come near us again. If I even hear of you thinking about us, I'll make it so you can't think at all."

The police officers came into the room with guns pointed. They cuffed Lukas after pulling Shane off him. That was all right with Shane. He had someone else who needed him.

Justin sat in the back of an ambulance with an EMT checking his vitals. Shane walked up with his hands in his pockets. Gone was the man who was sure of himself. There was sorrow and pain on Shane's face.

"I'm sorry." They spoke in unison. Smiles spread across their faces.

Climbing from the ambulance, Justin pushed the EMT away and walked straight into Shane's arms. He looked up. "Are you okay?"

"Me? I'm not the one who was being held hostage by a jealous drug addict," Shane said. "Are *you* okay?"

"Yeah, I'm good," Justin said. His heart was hammering a little harder than necessary and his appetite was gone, but other than that, he was fine. Mentally, the jury was still out. "Did you mean it? What you said back there?"

"Which part?" Shane grinned. He knew which part, damn it.

"Asshole." Justin smirked. "I love you too."

EPILOGUE

"Justin! Hurry up! You're going to be late." Shane checked his watch for the fifth time.

"I'm coming. Don't get your undies in a twist." Justin rushed in, snatched a kiss from Shane, and zoomed out the door. "Well, are you coming?"

Shane narrowed his eyes and growled as he locked the door behind them. "I'm going to beat your ass later."

"Yay me!" Justin laughed and climbed into Shane's car. He fidgeted in his seat until Shane got in and started the engine. "Pleasedon'tletmefallonmyface...."

"What?"

"Oh. I said, please don't let me fall on my face." Justin grinned and shrugged. "Grace under pressure isn't really me."

"You'll be fine. Just put one foot in front of the other and take your time." Shane reached over to squeeze Justin's hand. "And if you trip, tuck and roll."

"Ha-ha. You're so funny. It's a good thing you're cute...,"

Justin snarked, but Shane could see the smile he tried to hide.

"Oh yeah? Only cute? That's not what you said last night." Shane grinned. "You know? When you were trying to climb all over me."

"I did no such thing! I'm innocent, I tell ya." Justin nodded.

Shane snorted. "Sure you are."

They pulled into the college parking lot and found a spot. Shane turned off the car and turned to face Justin. "You'll be fine. I'm very proud of you. I don't know if I've told you that lately, but I am."

Justin's face softened before he leaned in to kiss Shane. "I love you."

"I love you too. Now go, so you can get lined up or whatever it is you're doing. I'll be as close to the front as I can get." Shane smiled.

"Okay. I'll see you soon." Justin climbed out of the car and scurried toward the front door of the school.

Shane left his car and headed to the auditorium where the ceremony was being held. Empty seats were spotty, but he found three together and only a handful of rows from the front. He pulled out his phone to check the view from there. He'd promised Justin a picture when he accepted his degree. Finishing college had been a long time coming, and Shane was proud of Justin's accomplishment.

More people came in until the auditorium was full. Voices talking at a whisper were amplified until it sounded like every person was shouting. Shane bounced his knee, then tapped his toe, and then went back to bouncing his knee. He checked the time—the ceremony should be starting any minute. He looked up and back toward the entrance.

Justin's parents were standing there. Shane stood and waved to get their attention.

Mrs. Walker reached him first and wrapped her arms around him. "How was he?"

"Nervous about tripping, but okay otherwise," Shane said.

She pulled back so her husband could shake Shane's hand. "Good to see you, son."

"Thank you, sir. It's good to see you as well." He smiled.

"Let's sit down. The ceremony should be about ready to begin." Mrs. Walker moved around Shane to take the seat next to his.

The commencement music filtered through the speakers, and people rose from their seats. Shane stood too, his hands folded in front of him. As the graduates made their way down the middle aisle, he looked for the familiar face in line. He caught Justin's eye and winked. Justin smiled in return, finger waving from where his hand hung by his sides.

Shane mouthed, "Tuck and roll," making Justin laugh. He was so freaking proud he wanted to point and shout *He's mine.*

The students took their seats, and the speakers started. Shane videoed all of it with his phone.

Finally it came time to present the diplomas. One by one, names were called and the graduates stepped up onto the stage. Shane whistled when Justin's name was called. *Please don't let him trip.*

Shane took a picture when Justin smiled toward the audience, and then he whistled again when Justin was handed his diploma. Seeing the pride and happiness on Justin's face instead of terror relieved Shane. Even more so when Justin made it across the stage and back to his seat without incident.

After the ceremony was over, Shane and Justin's parents found Justin. Shane hugged him so tight, he lifted him off the ground. "I'm so proud of you!"

With a rosy glow on his cheeks and a mile-wide grin, Justin returned his hug. "Thanks."

Justin's father shook his hand, and his mother hugged him, each echoing Shane's sentence.

"Thank you for being here," Justin said to his parents.

"Justin? A word, please?" A man walked up to them. Shane recognized him as one of the speakers but couldn't remember the man's name.

"Hi, Professor Chapman. These are my parents, Roger and Phyllis, and this is my boyfriend, Shane...."

"Nice to meet you," Professor Chapman said with a smile. He turned toward Justin. "I have news for you."

"Good news, I hope," Justin said.

"I think it is," the professor said. "I just heard from a friend on the city council. A youth center is opening downtown, and they need qualified bodies. I gave him your contact information. You should hear from him in the next few days."

"Oh my God! Thank you!"

Shane waited for Justin to start jumping up and down with excitement. He'd talked about nothing else since Professor Chapman had told the class about the possibility.

"Nothing to thank me for, but you're welcome." He chuckled, shook hands with Justin, Shane, and Justin's parents, then wandered away.

"Oh my God! Did you hear that?" Justin's voice rose about three octaves.

Shane grinned. "I did. Congratulations!"

"We have to celebrate."

"Already ahead of you. Let's go.... Unless you want to mingle more?" Shane asked.

"Nah, I'm good. I just want to spend the rest of the night with you," Justin said.

"You're in luck. I happen to be free."

"Your mother and I would like to take Shane and you out to dinner next weekend, if you're able?" Justin's father asked.

Justin looked at Shane, who nodded and smiled. "We'd love to."

"Great! I'll call you when I have the reservations made, honey." His mother kissed Justin's cheek and stepped back. "Go. Have fun and we'll see you later."

Shane winked at Mrs. Walker, who knew his plans, and threw his arm around Justin's shoulders to lead them away from the crowd.

Little did Justin know, but Shane had their bags packed and tickets ready for a weekend of drag racing at the NHRA New England Nationals in New Hampshire. It would be a short trip, but Justin deserved the vacation after busting his butt to graduate at the top of his class. A wedding at the Christmas tree seemed like the perfect beginning of their lives together.... The arrangements were all made, and Shane couldn't wait to see Justin's face.

ABOUT THE AUTHOR

Tracey Michael is the pen name of Tracey Steinbach. Her three children call her Mom or Mama. Tracey has been married for over twenty years to a man who's broadened her horizons. He introduced her to NHRA Drag Racing in 1997. She's been a fan ever since.

Tracey has an eclectic taste in music, enjoying everything from country to hard rock. Def Leppard is her favorite rock band.

Tracey enjoys watching Disney cartoon movies, action/adventure, and romantic comedies. She's a huge Marvel and Harry Potter fan.

She loves watching NFL Football. Go 9ers and Saints!

Tracey has been an avid reader since her teen years. She started writing, seriously, after her first short story was accepted for an anthology in 2011. Reading books for a living had always been a dream of Tracey's. She often jokes that she writes to fund her reading habit.

Readers and fans are always welcome to contact Tracey on Facebook.

Blog: traceysteinbachtraceymichael.blogspot.com
Website: traceysteinbachmichael.webs.com